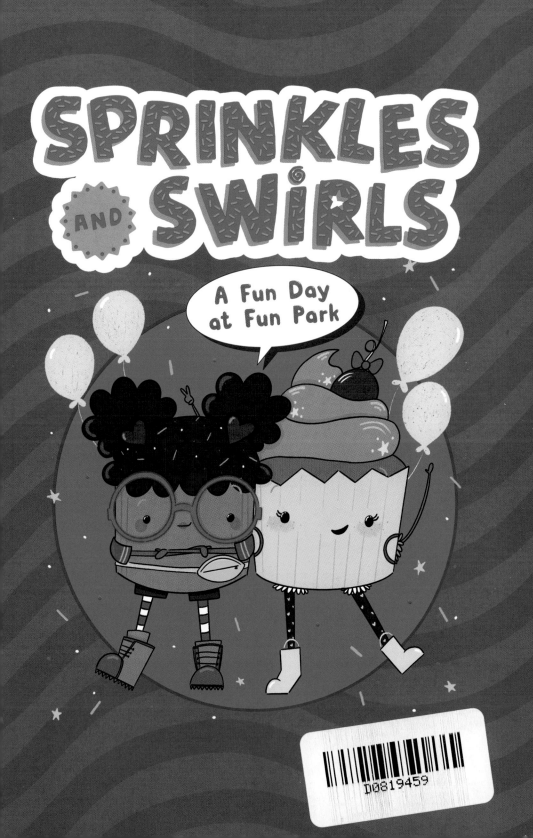

SPRINKLES AND SWIRLS

A Fun Day
at Fun Park

D0819459

For Lennon, the happiest cupcake of all! —L. S.

For Kramer, Sadie Lou, Baby Ben, Christy, and Gabrielle—
thank you for everything! —S. A.

SIMON SPOTLIGHT
An imprint of Simon & Schuster Children's Publishing Division
1230 Avenue of the Americas, New York, New York 10020
This Simon Spotlight edition December 2021
Text copyright © 2021 by Lola Schaefer
Illustrations copyright © 2021 by Savannah Allen
For information about special discounts for bulk purchases, please contact Simon & Schuster Special
Sales at 1-866-506-1949 or business@simonandschuster.com.
Manufactured in the United States of America 1021 LAK
2 4 6 8 10 9 7 5 3 1
Cataloging-in-Publication Data for this title is available from the Library of Congress.
ISBN 978-1-6659-0329-5 (hc)
ISBN 978-1-6659-0328-8 (pbk)
ISBN 978-1-6659-0330-1 (ebook)

SPRINKLES AND SWIRLS

A Fun Day at Fun Park

Written by **LOLA M. SCHAEFER** ★ Illustrated by **SAVANNAH ALLEN**

Ready-to-Read *GRAPHICS*

Simon Spotlight

New York   London   Toronto   Sydney   New Delhi

HOW TO READ THIS BOOK

Sprinkles and Swirls are here to give you some tips on reading this book.

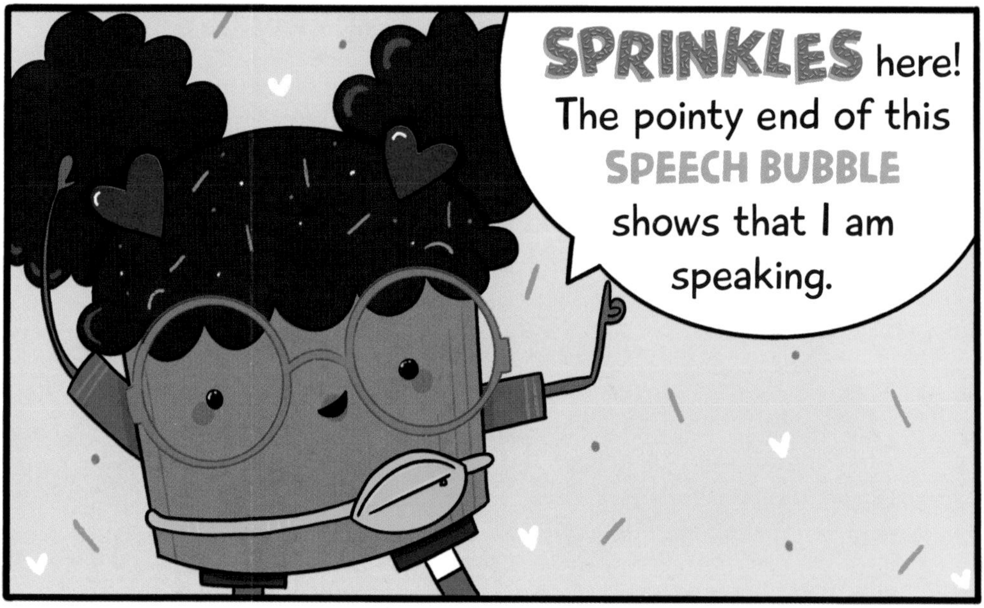
SPRINKLES here! The pointy end of this SPEECH BUBBLE shows that I am speaking.

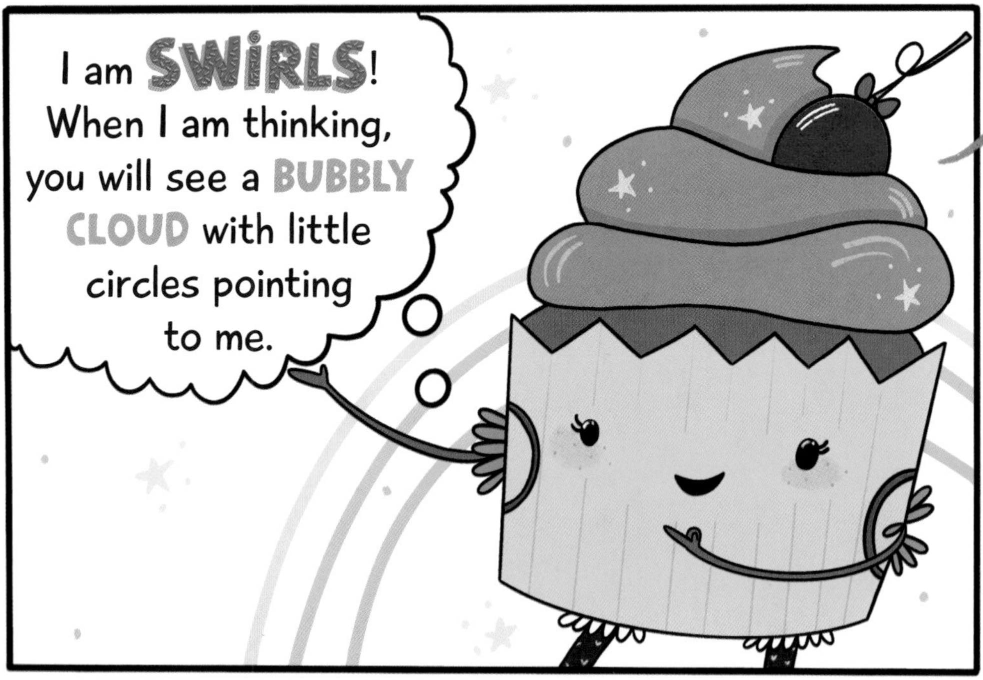
I am SWIRLS! When I am thinking, you will see a BUBBLY CLOUD with little circles pointing to me.

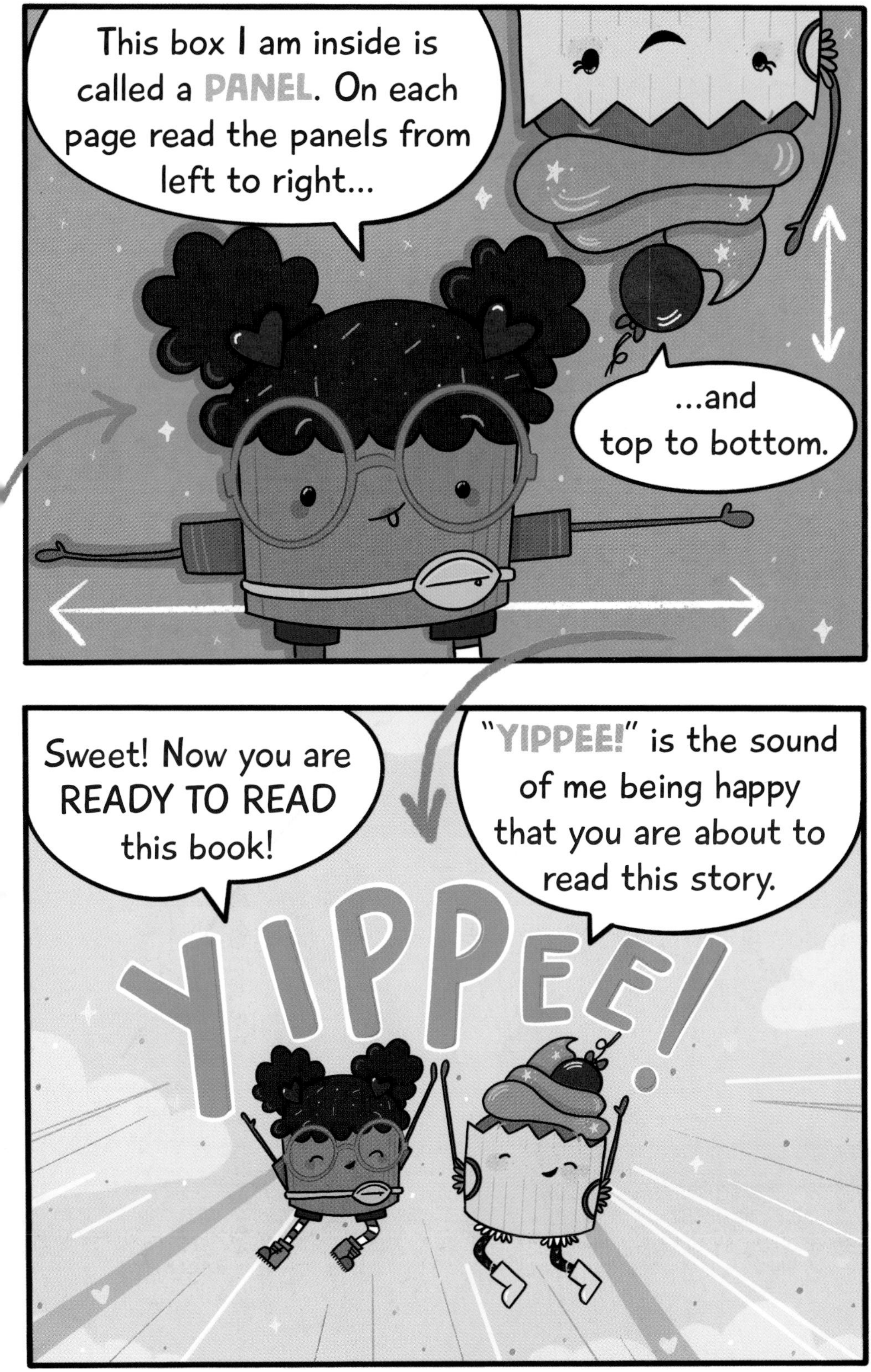
This box I am inside is called a PANEL. On each page read the panels from left to right...
...and top to bottom.
Sweet! Now you are READY TO READ this book!
"YIPPEE!" is the sound of me being happy that you are about to read this story.
YIPPEE!

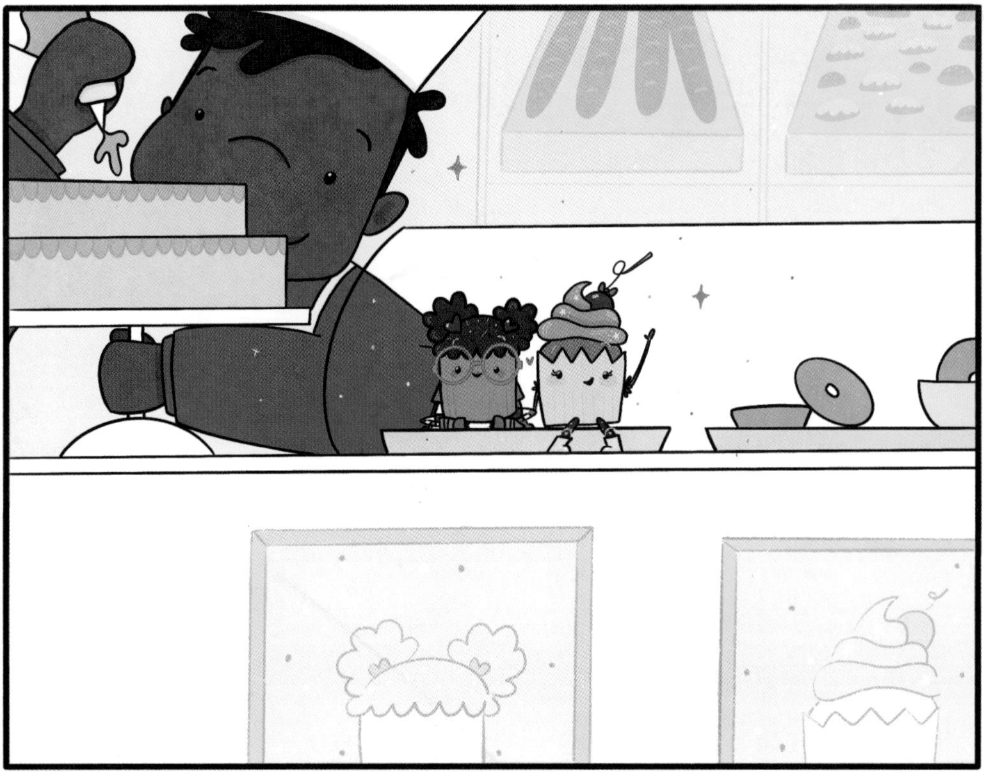

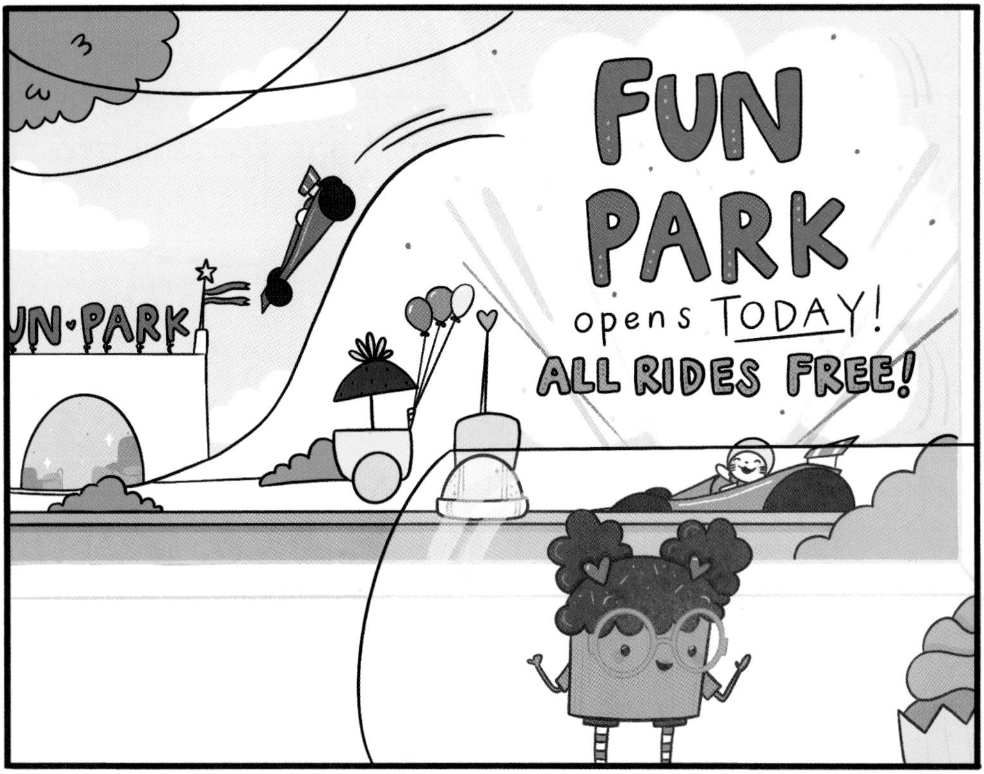
UN•PARK
FUN PARK
opens TODAY!
ALL RIDES FREE!

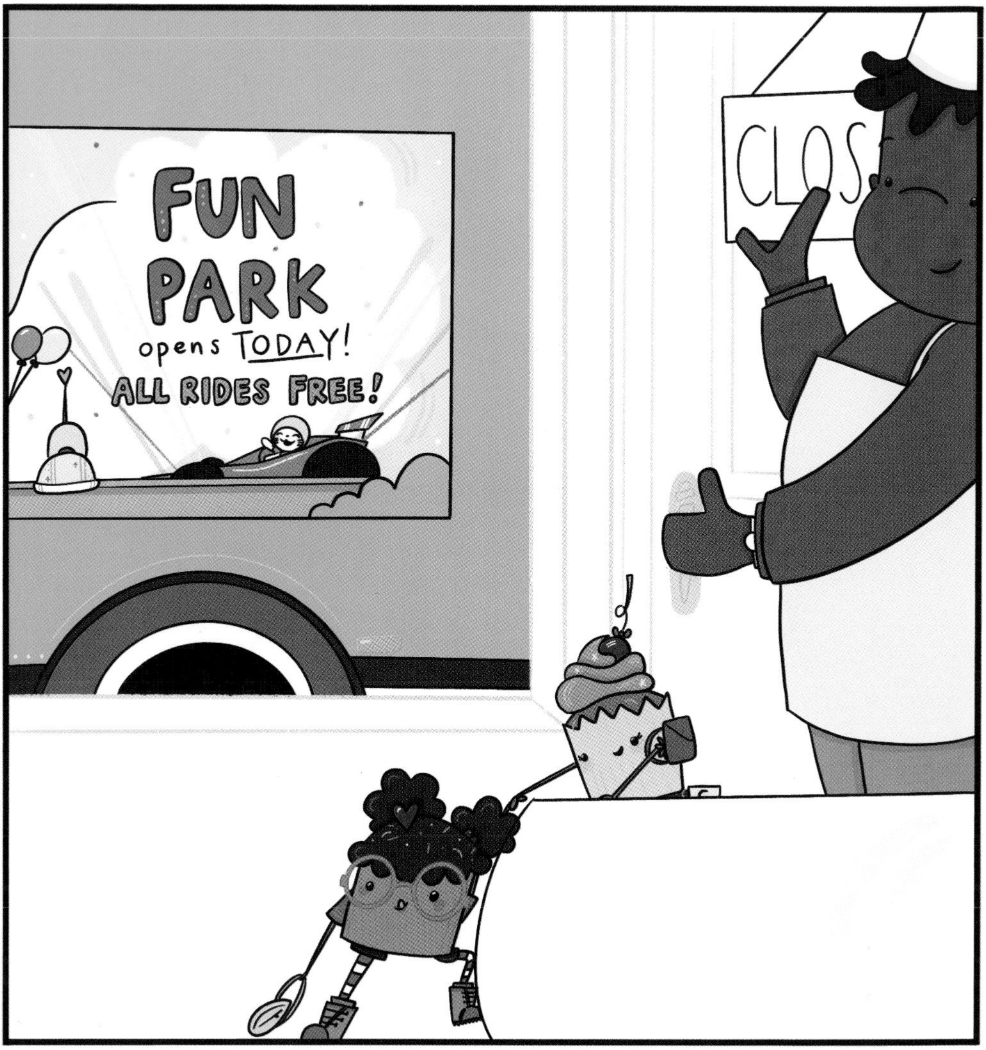
FUN
PARK
opens TODAY!
ALL RIDES FREE!
CLOS

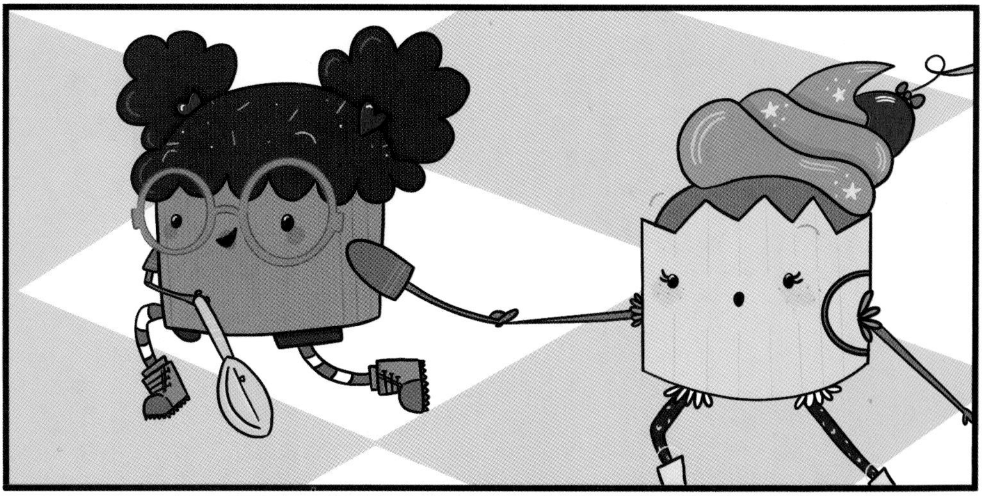

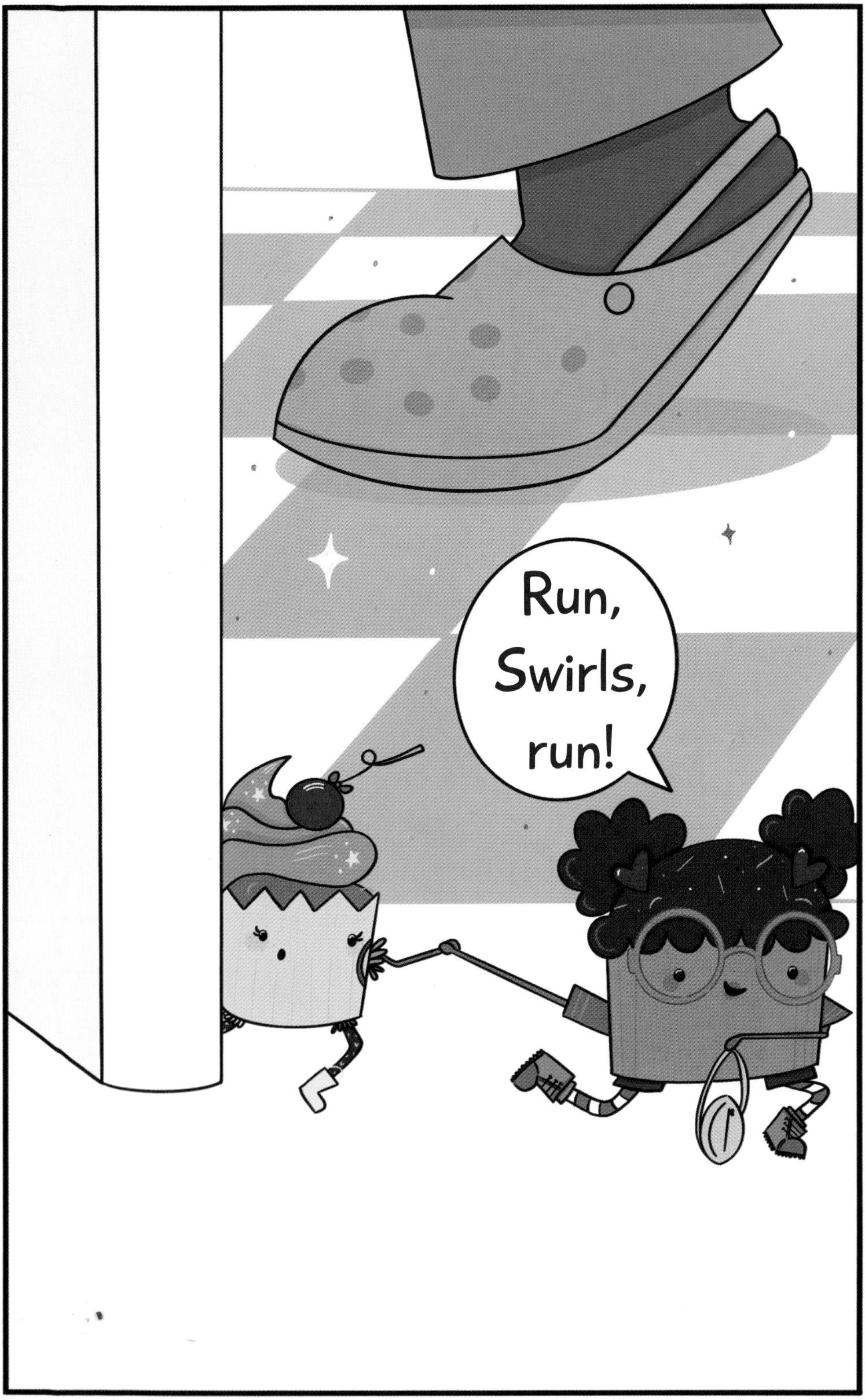
Run, Swirls, run!

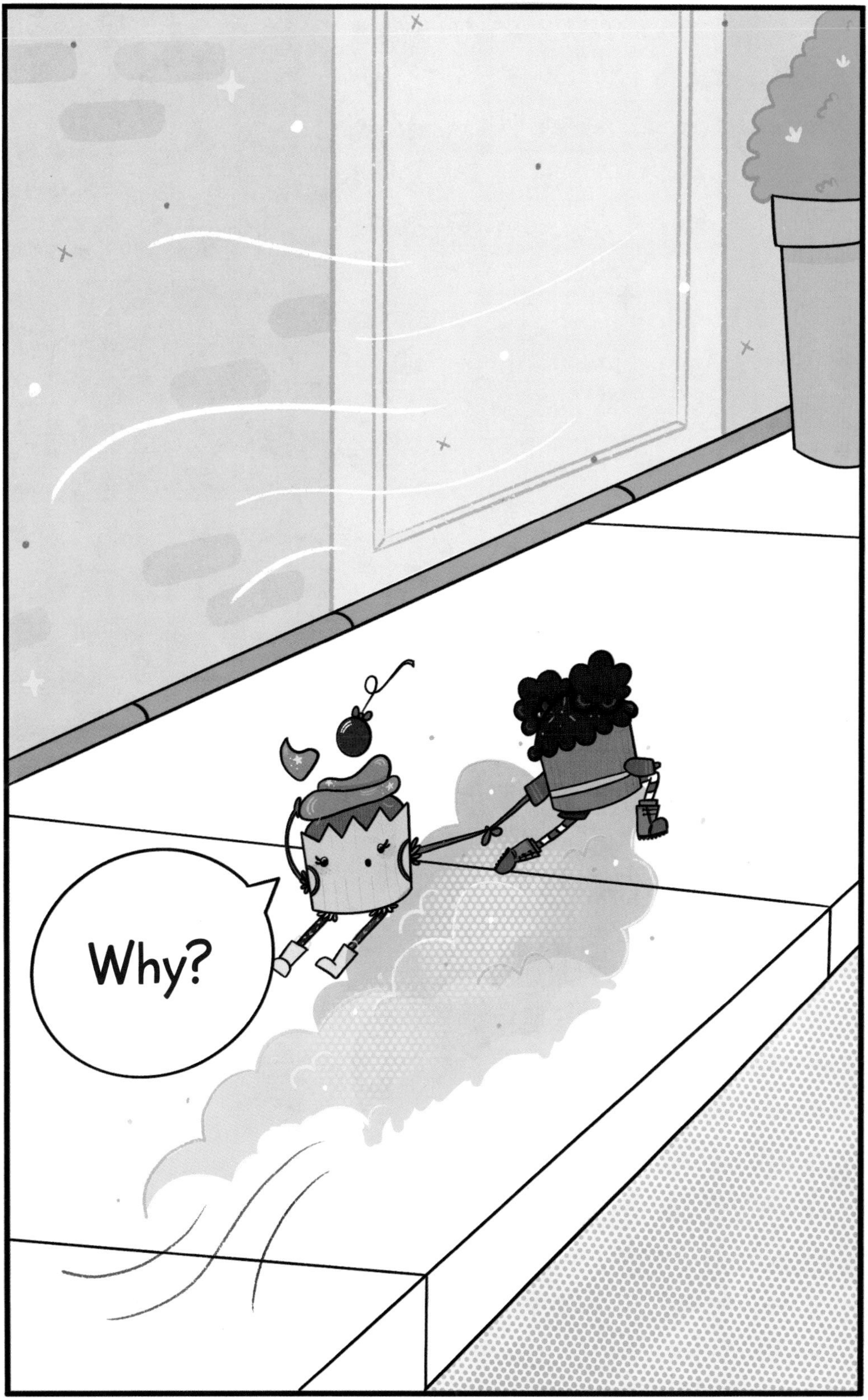
Why?

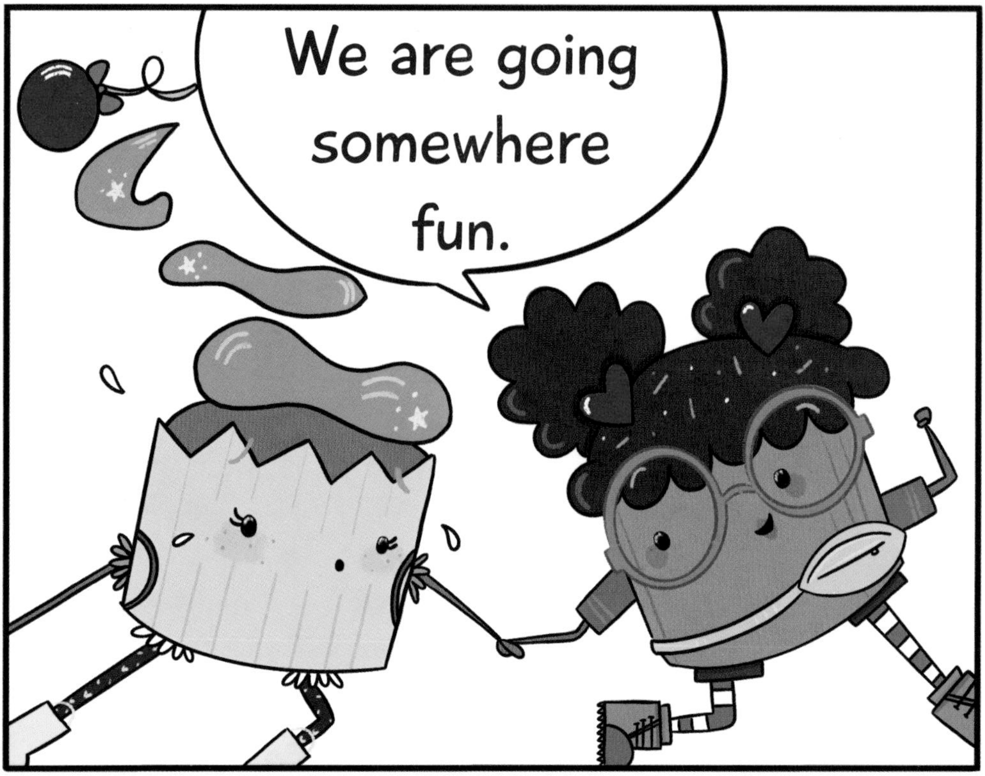
We are going somewhere fun.

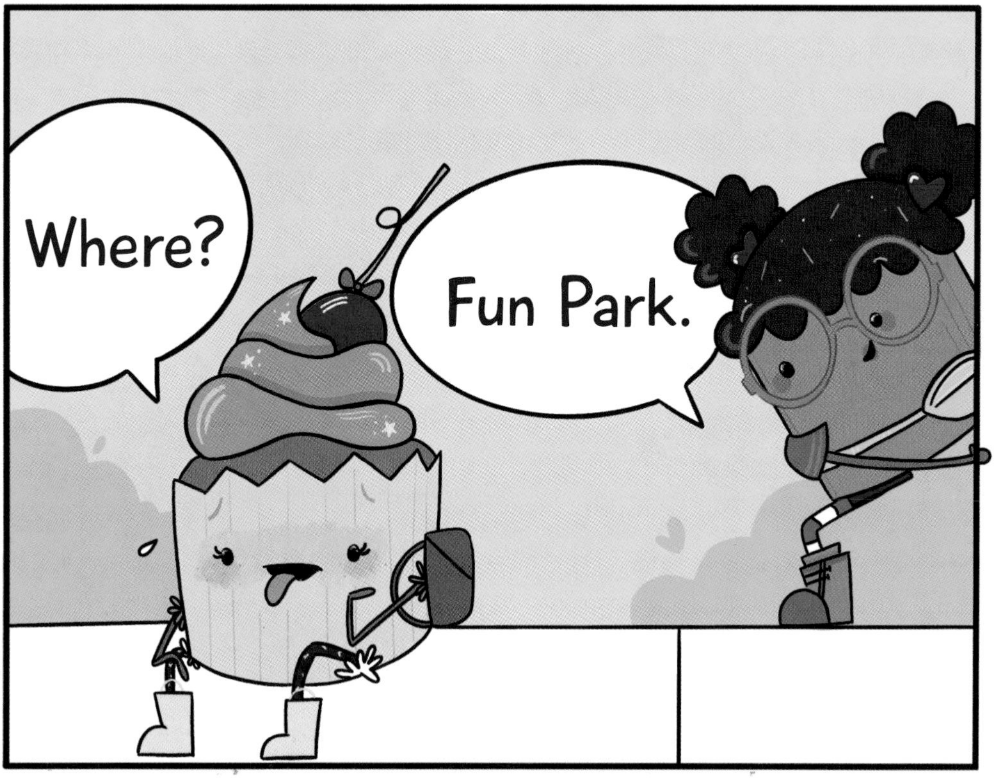
Where?
Fun Park.

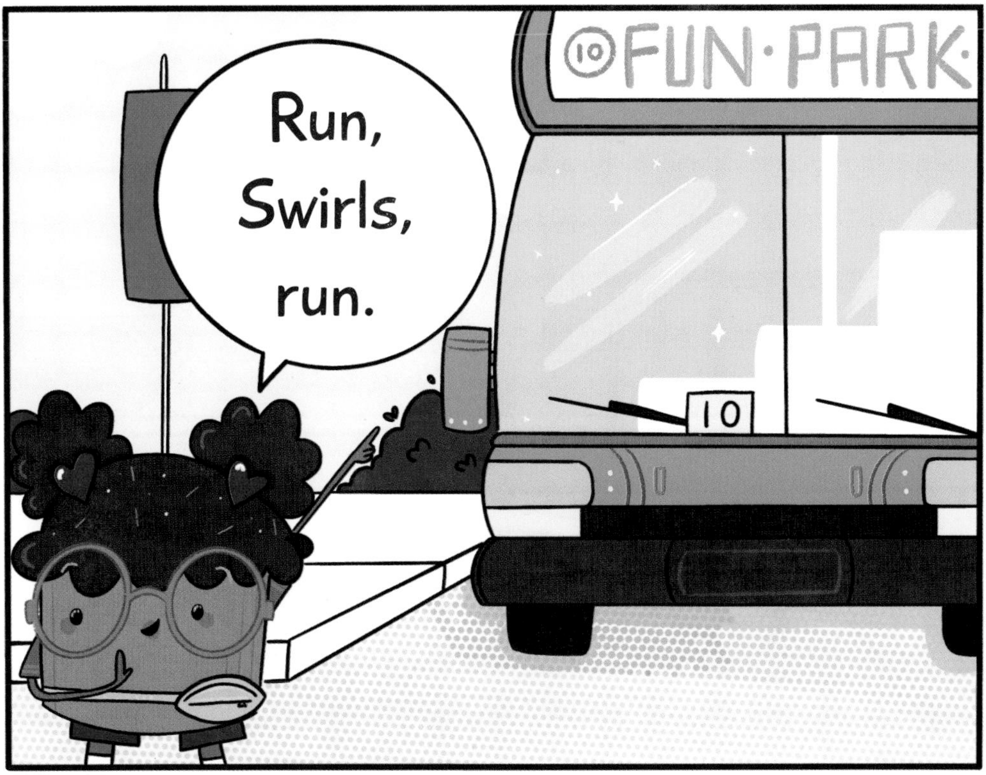
FUN · PARK
10
Run, Swirls, run.
10

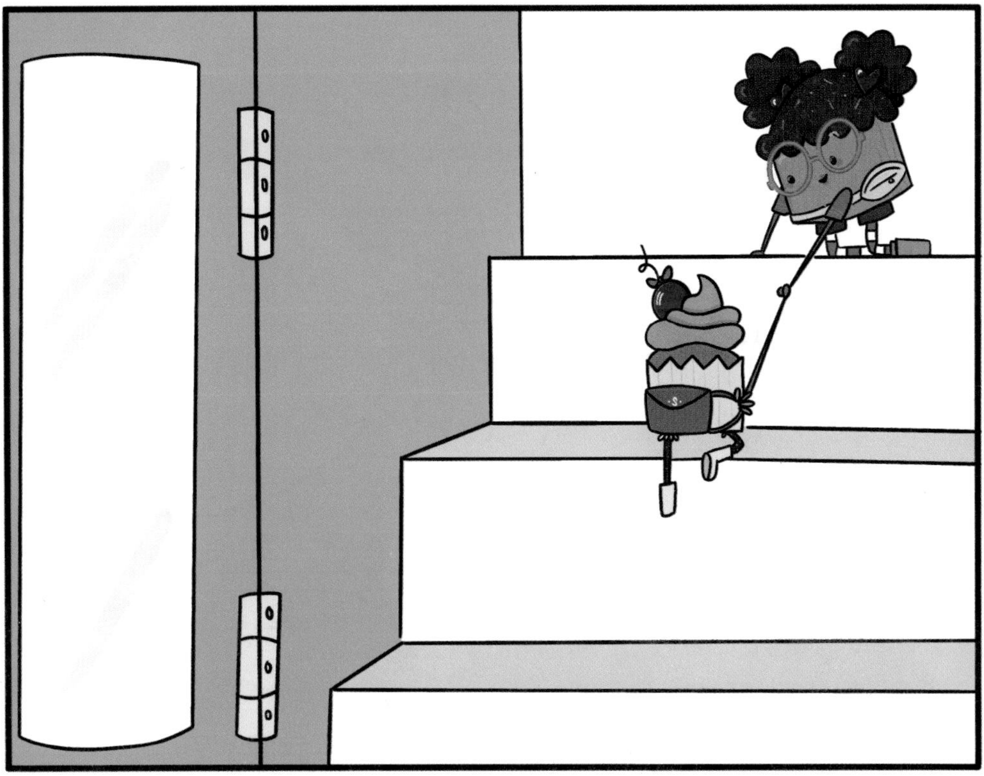

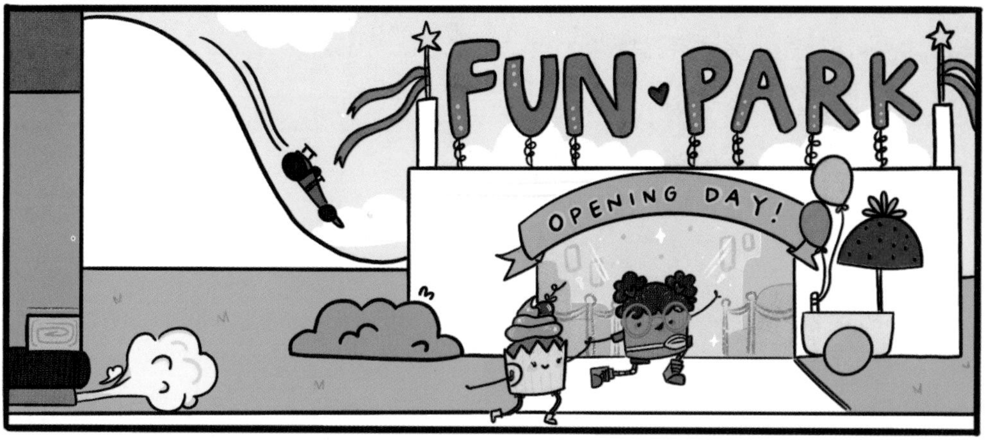
FUN·PARK
OPENING DAY!

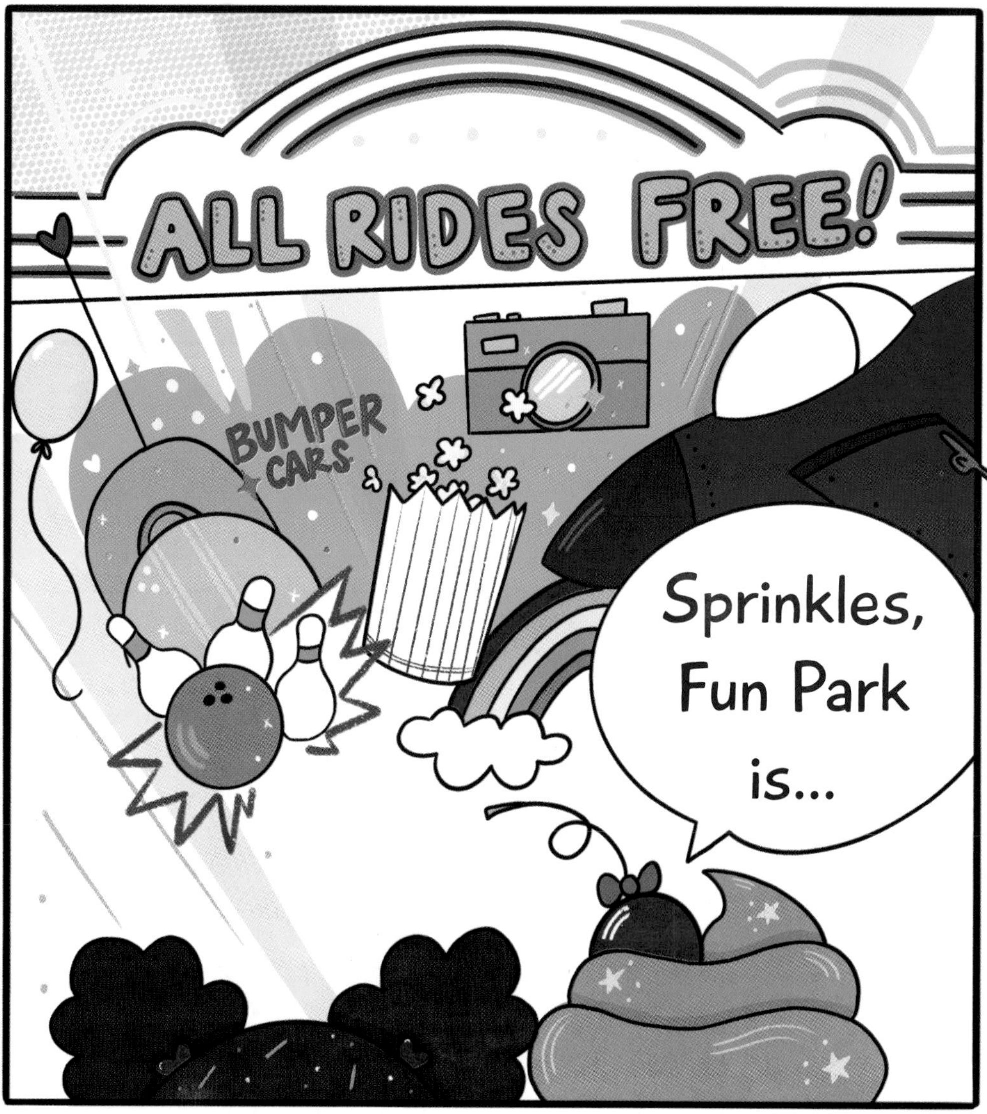
ALL RIDES FREE!
BUMPER CARS
Sprinkles, Fun Park is...

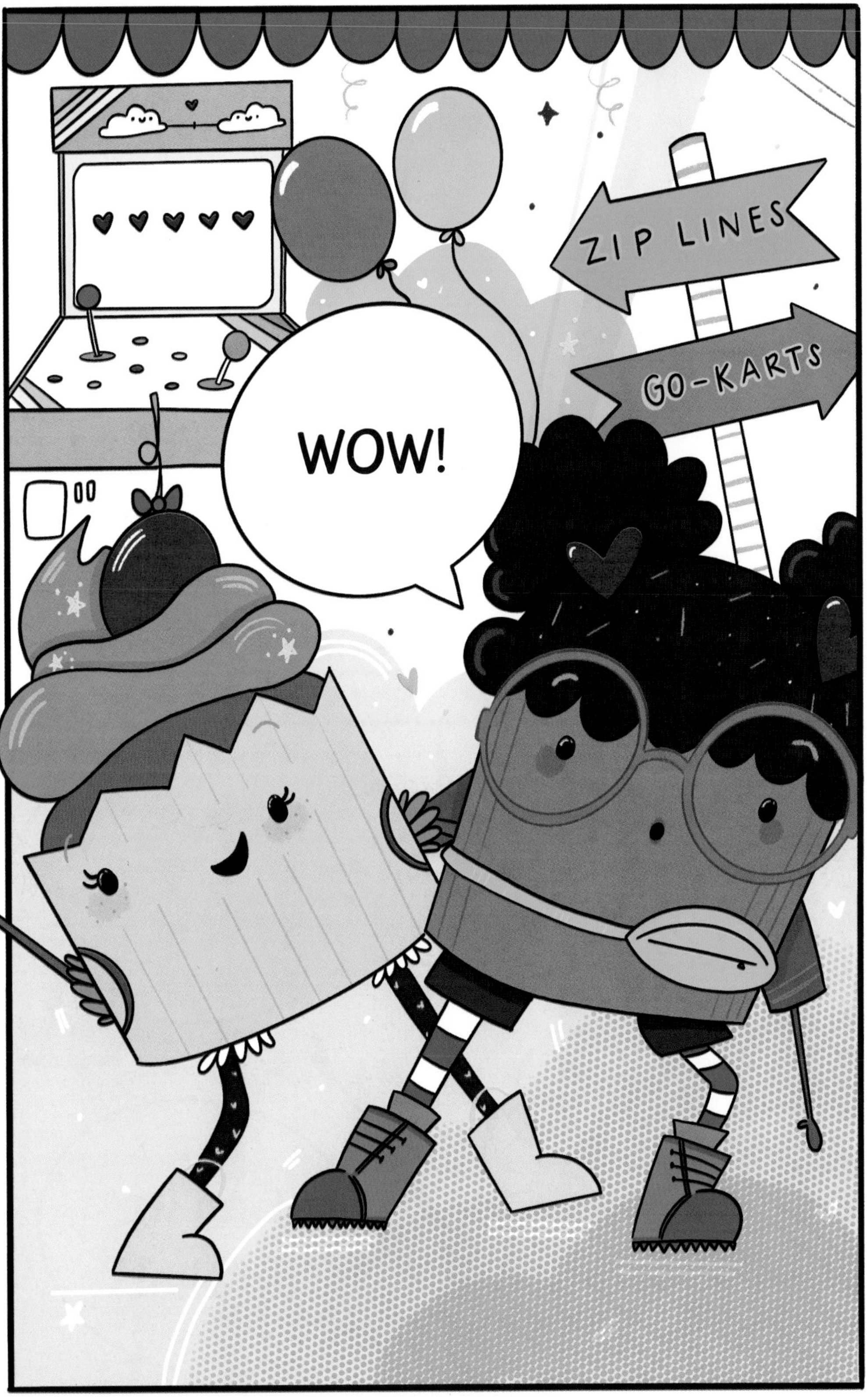
WOW!
ZIP LINES
GO-KARTS

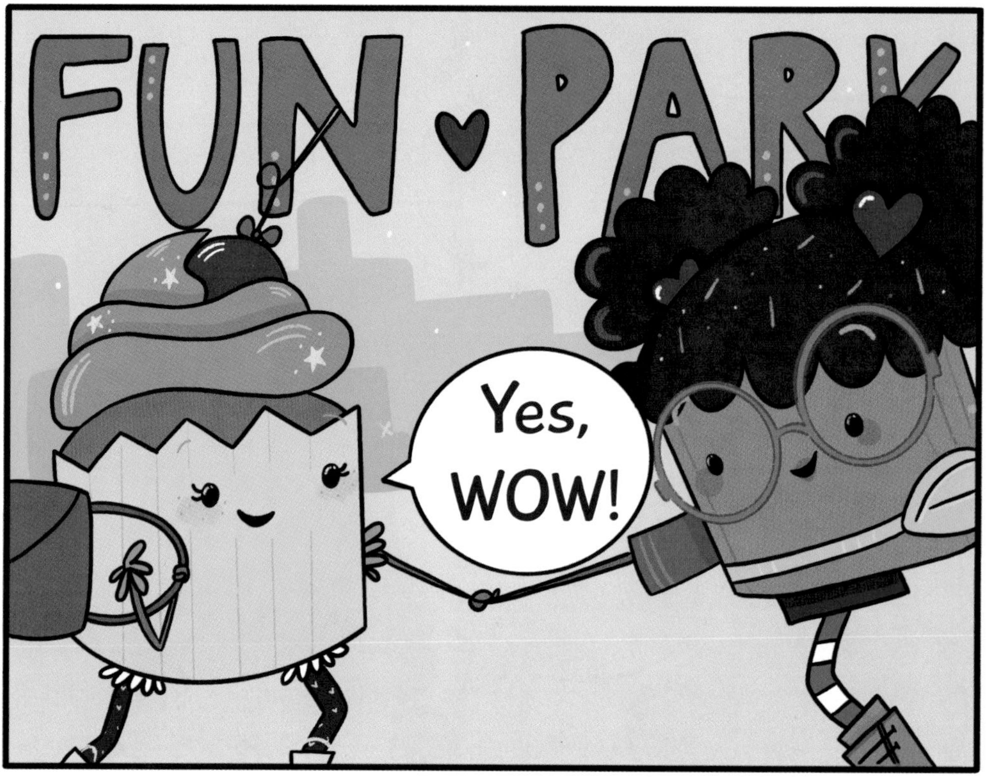
FUN PARK
Yes, WOW!

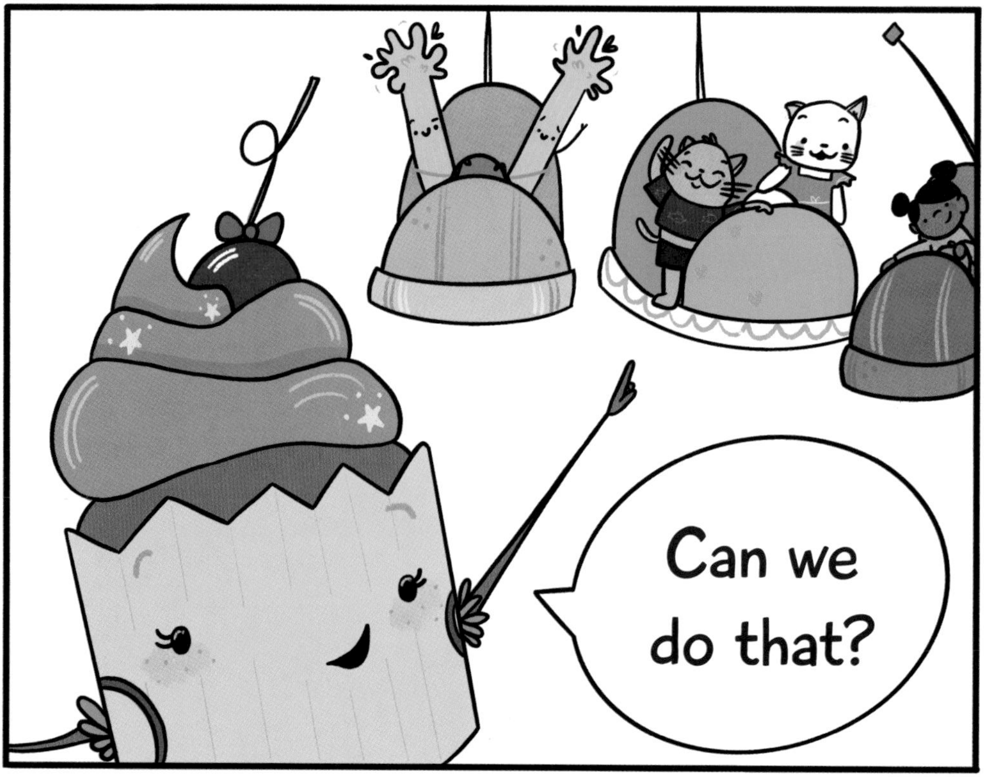
Can we do that?

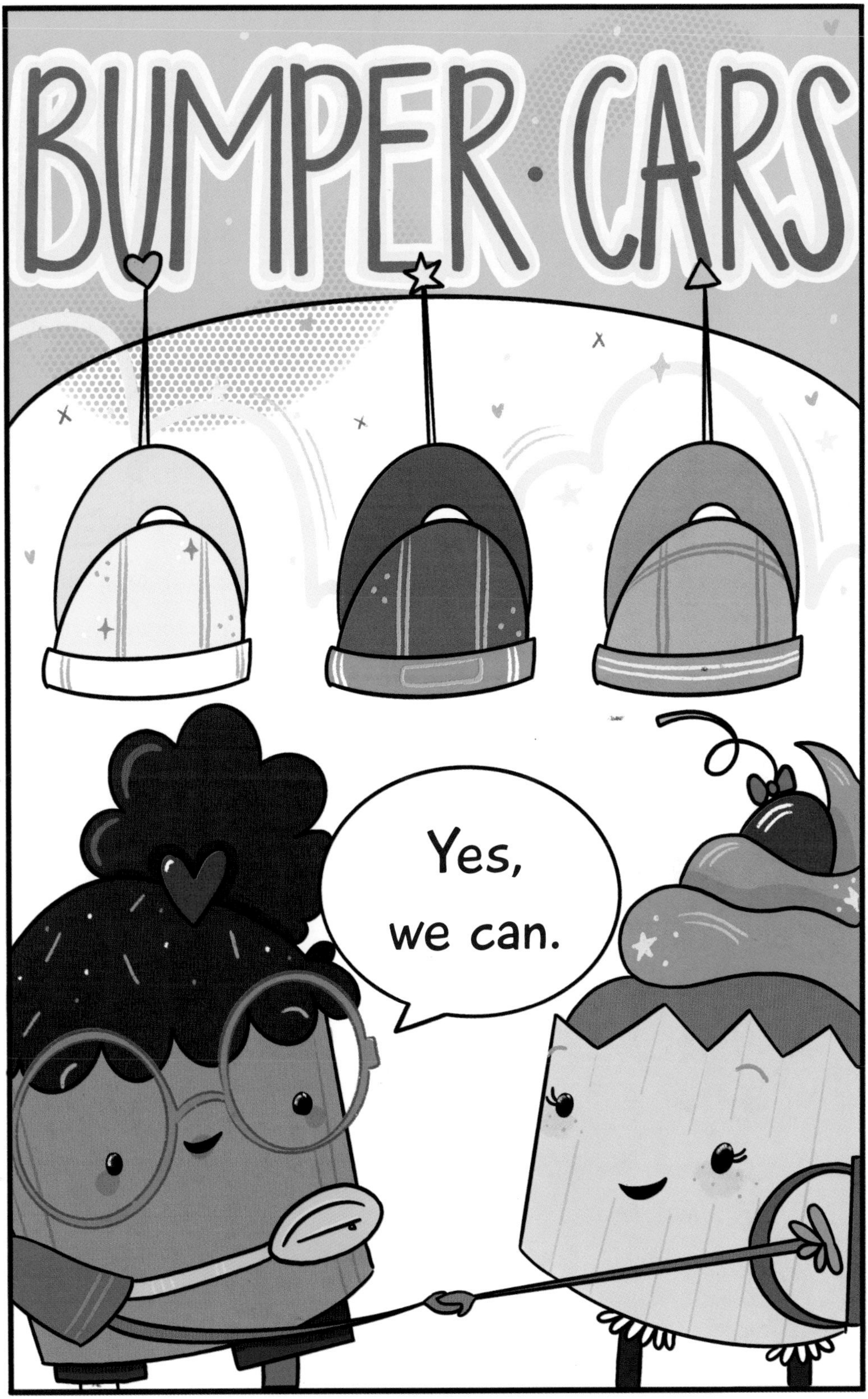
BUMPER CARS
Yes, we can.

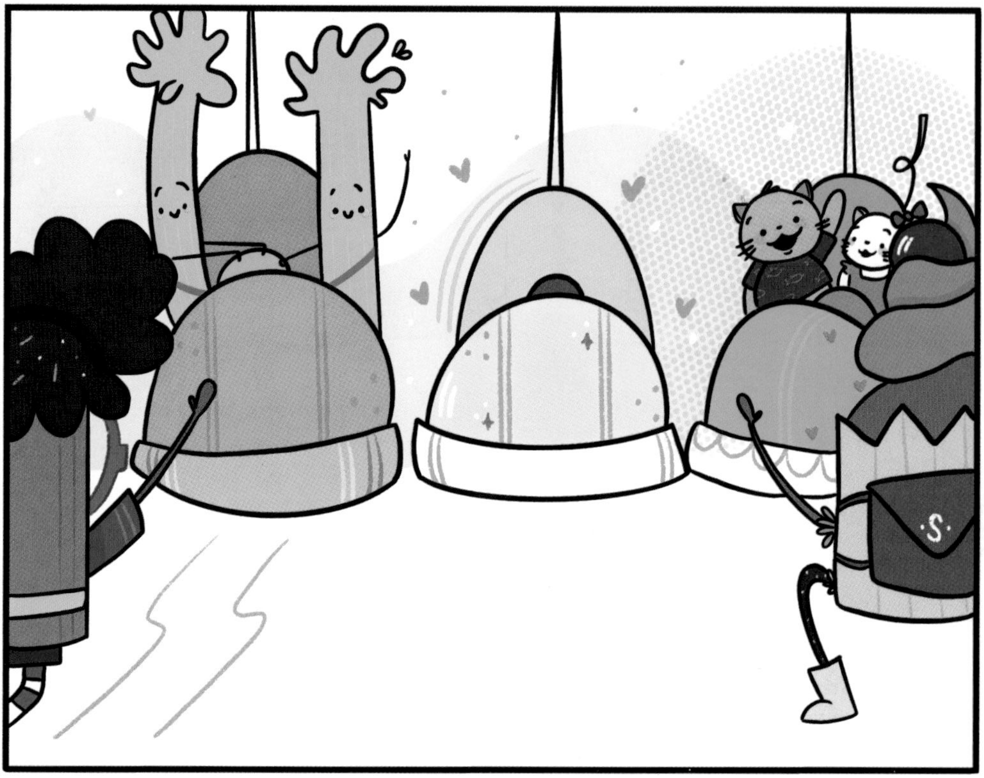

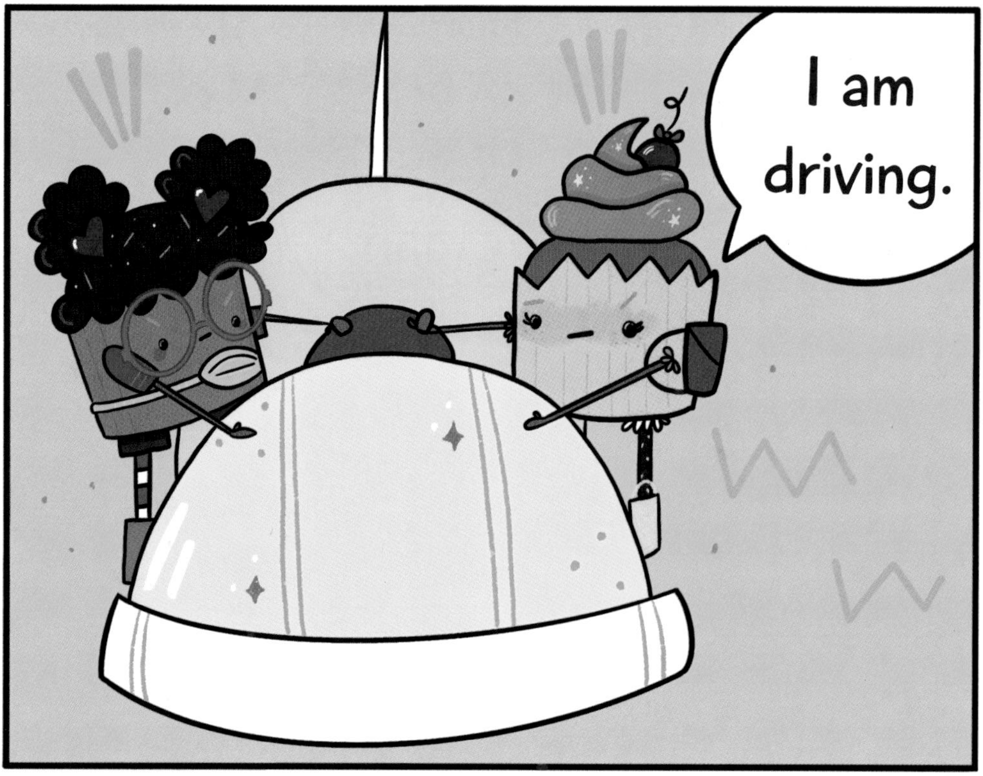
I am driving.

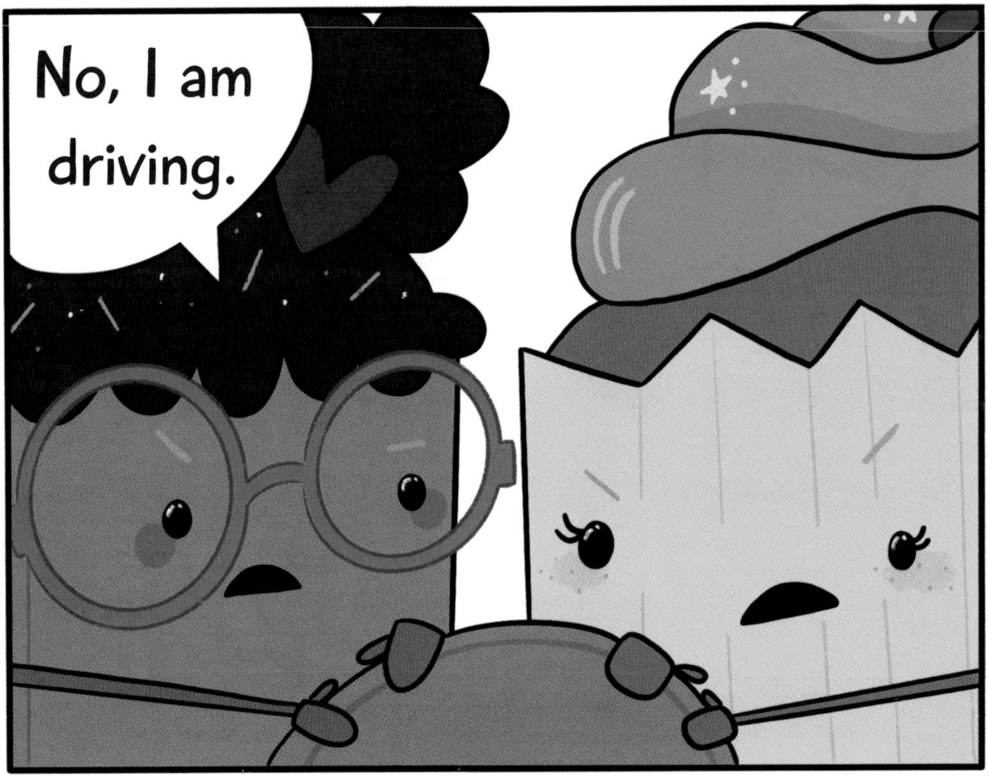
No, I am driving.

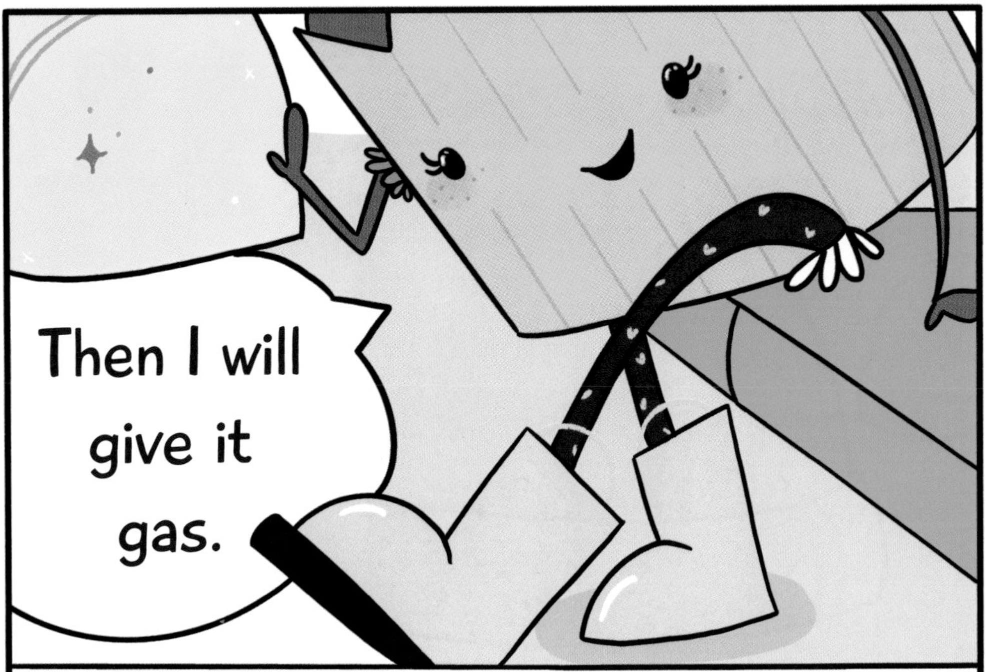
Then I will give it gas.

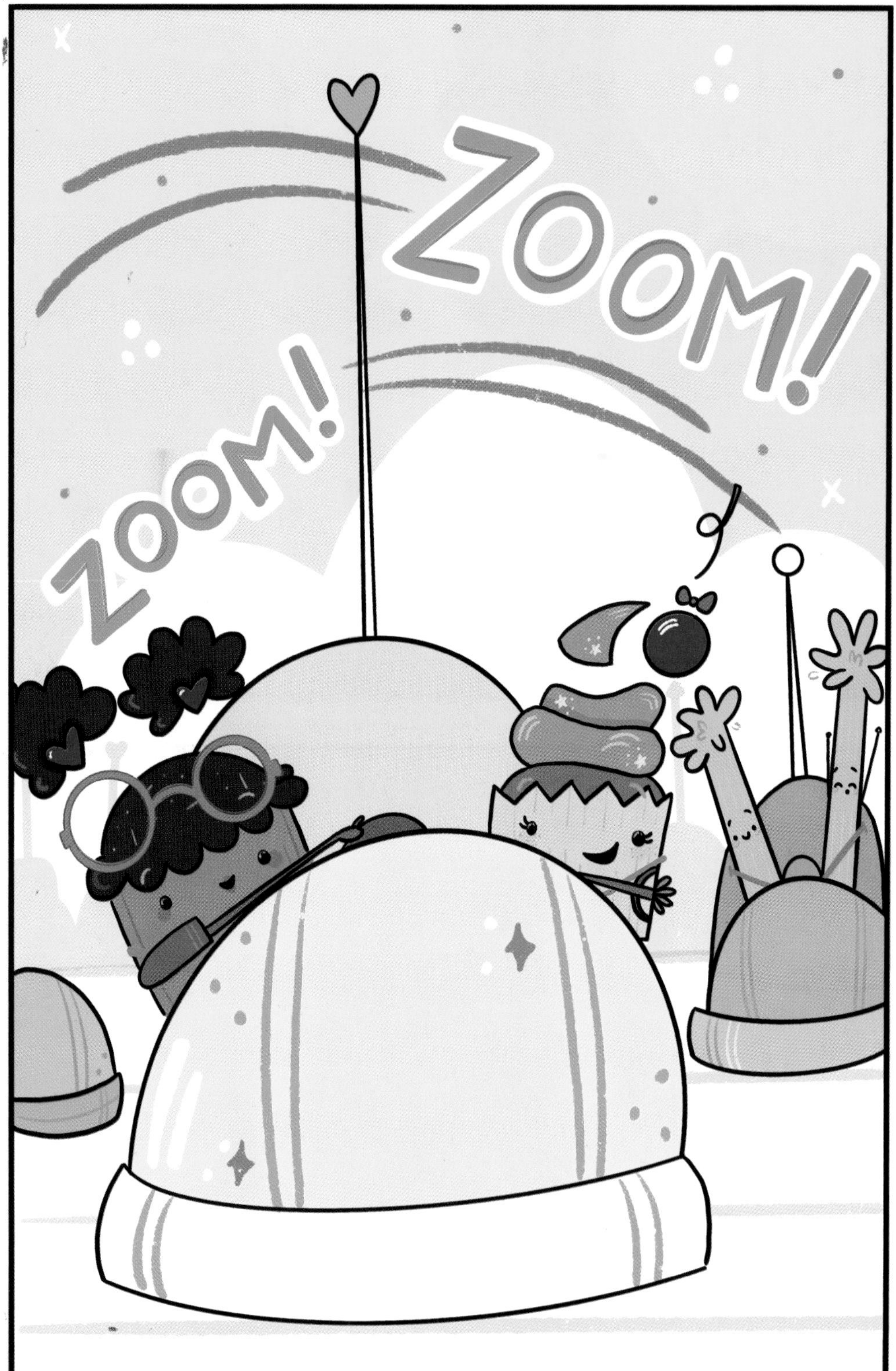
ZOOM!
ZOOM!

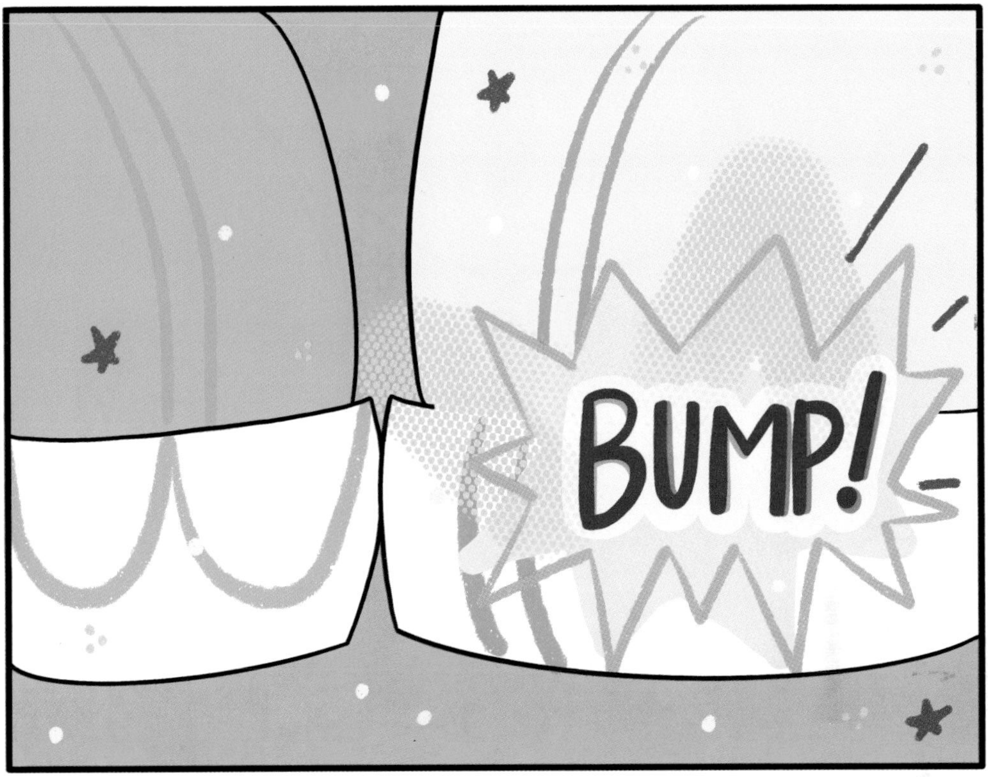
BUMP!

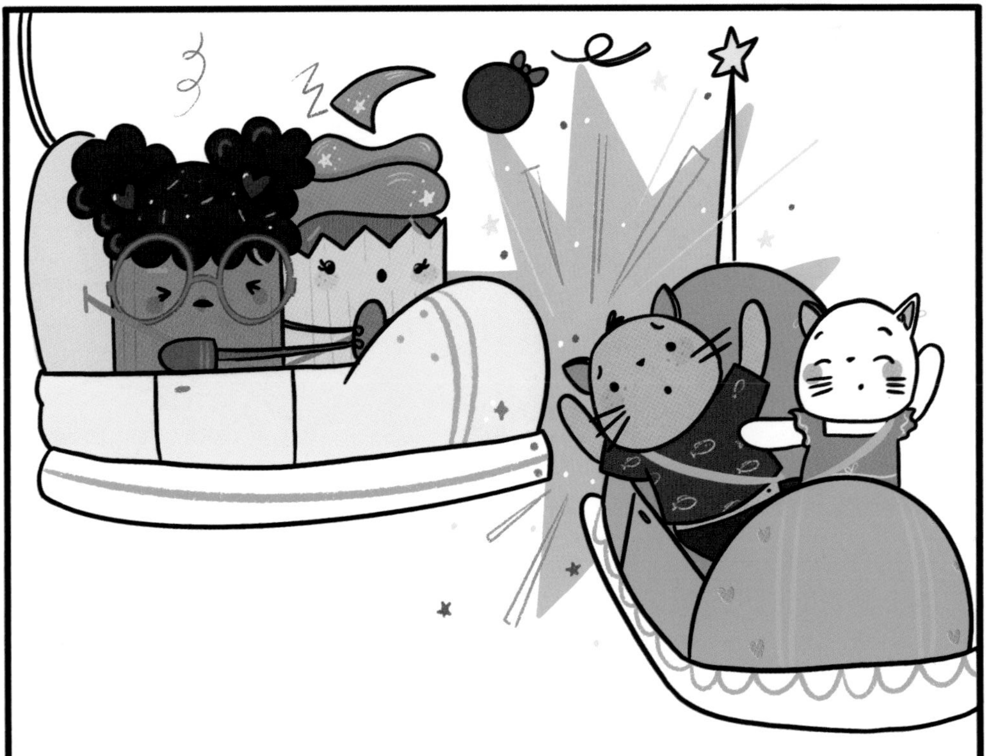

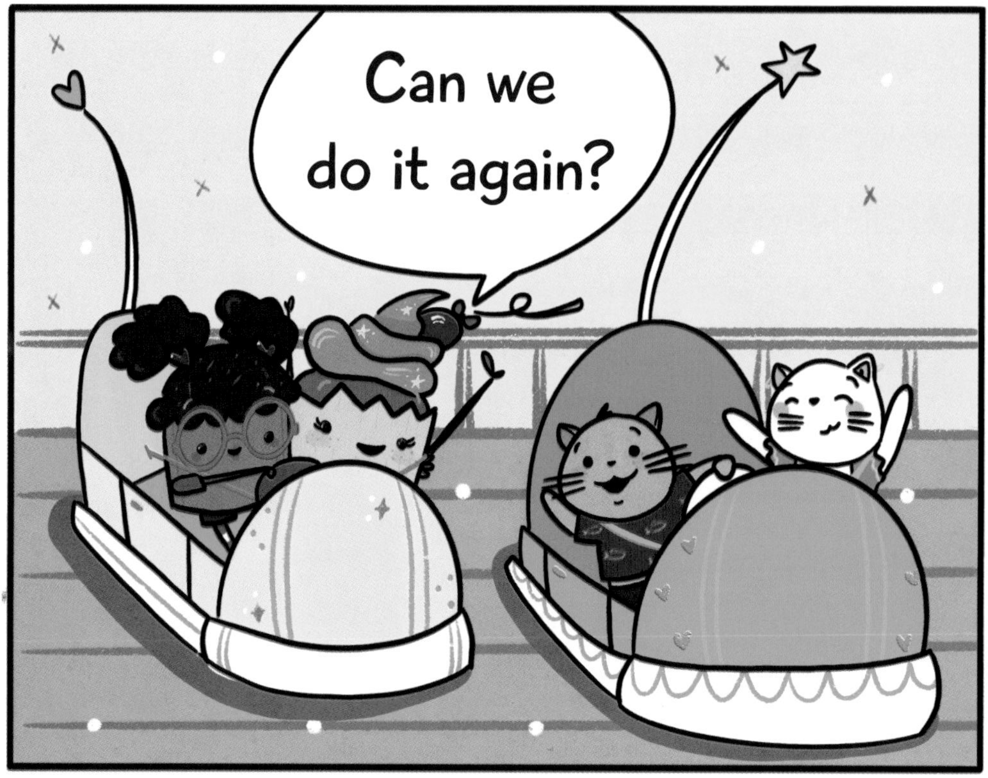
Can we do it again?

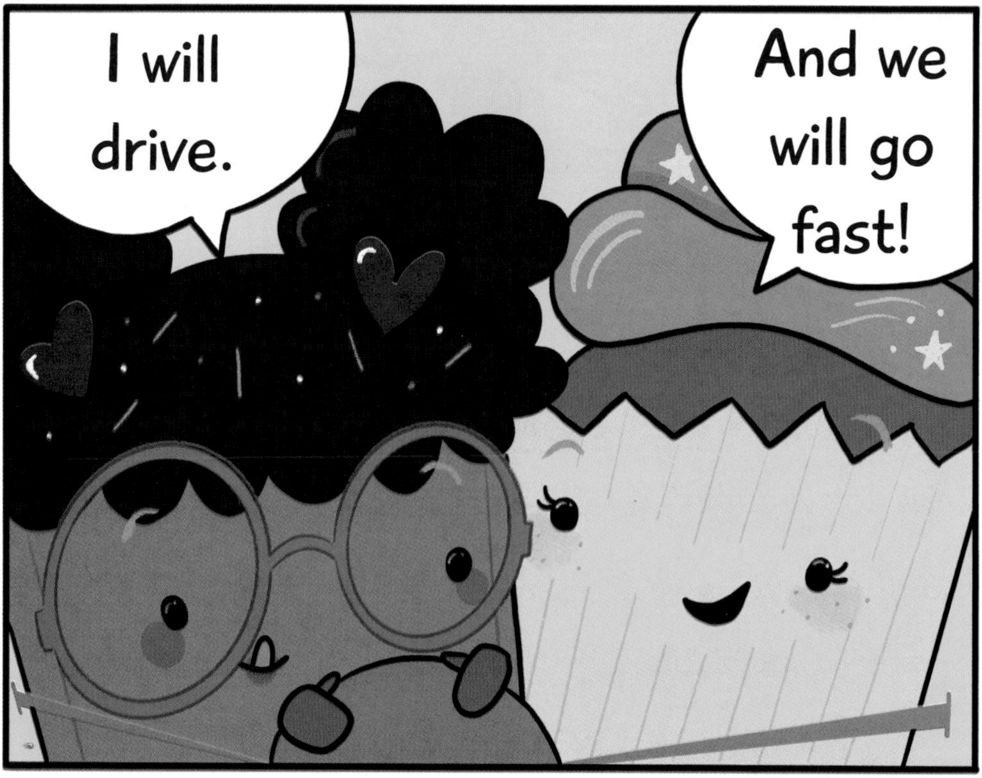
I will drive.
And we will go fast!

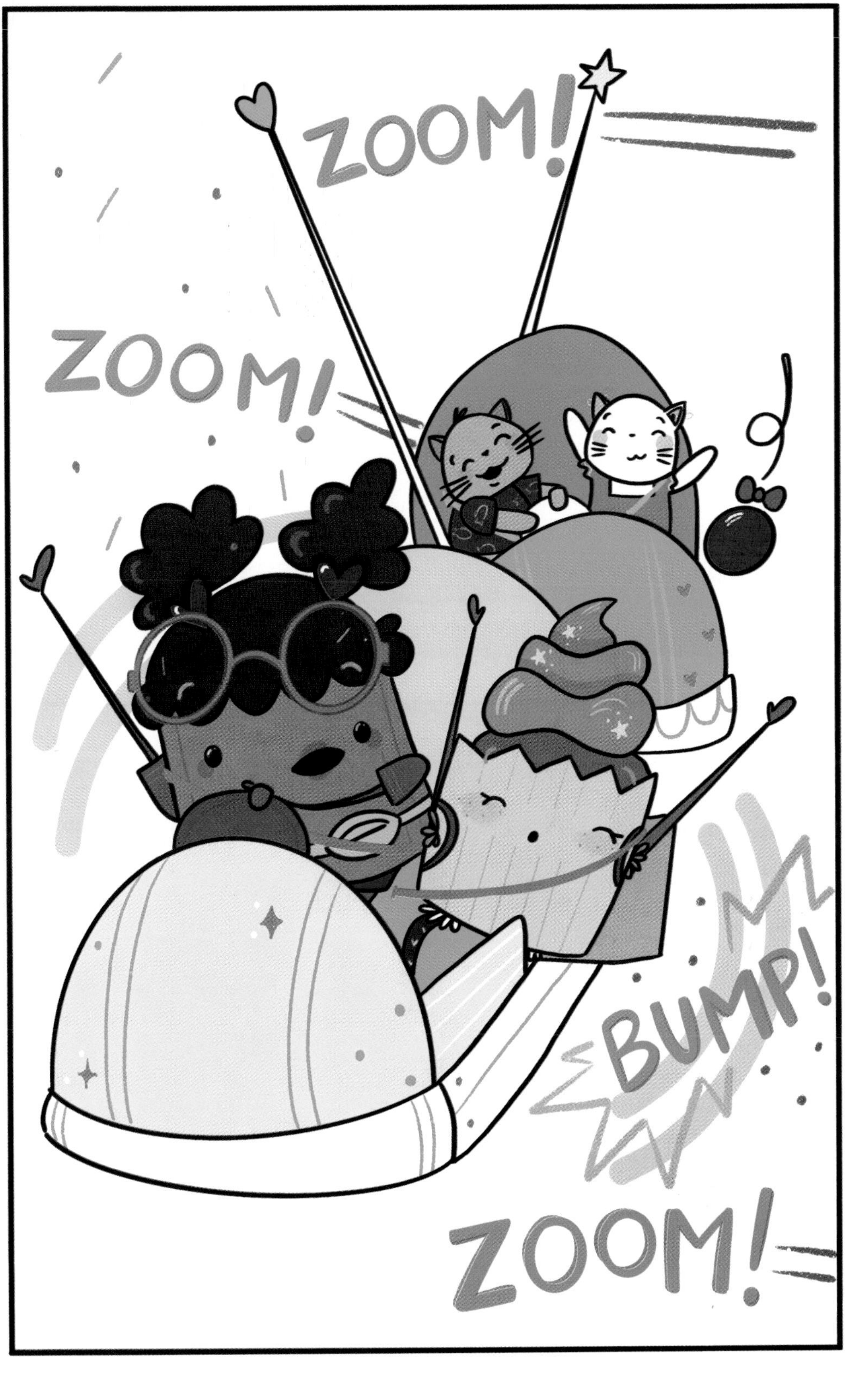
ZOOM!
ZOOM!
BUMP!
ZOOM!

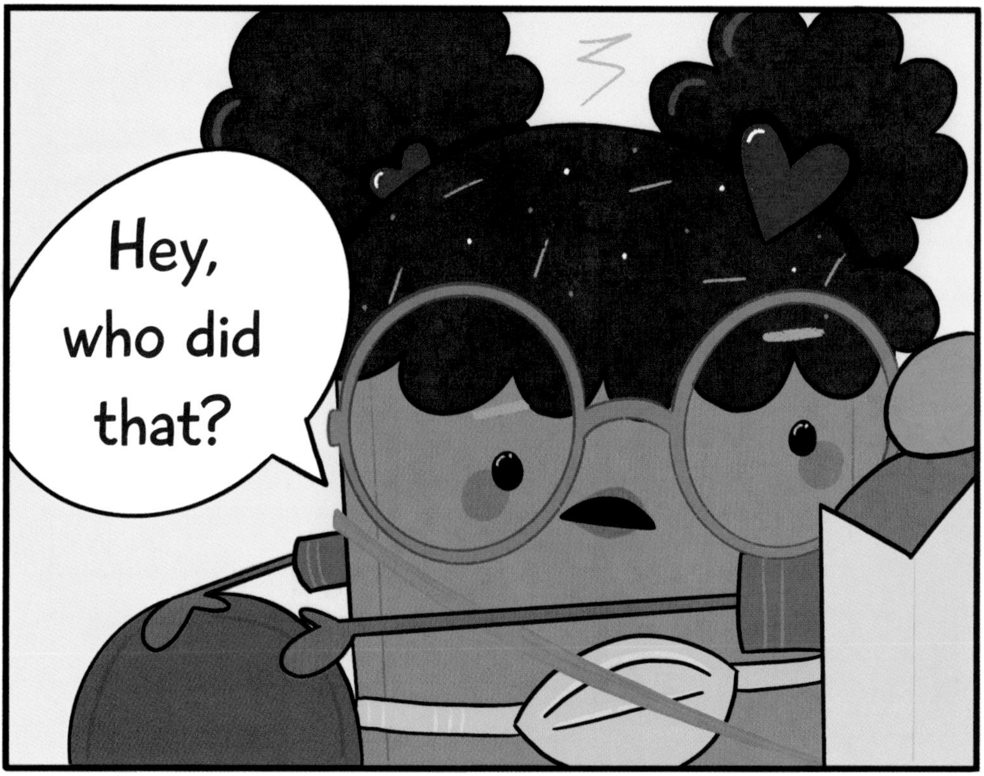
Hey, who did that?
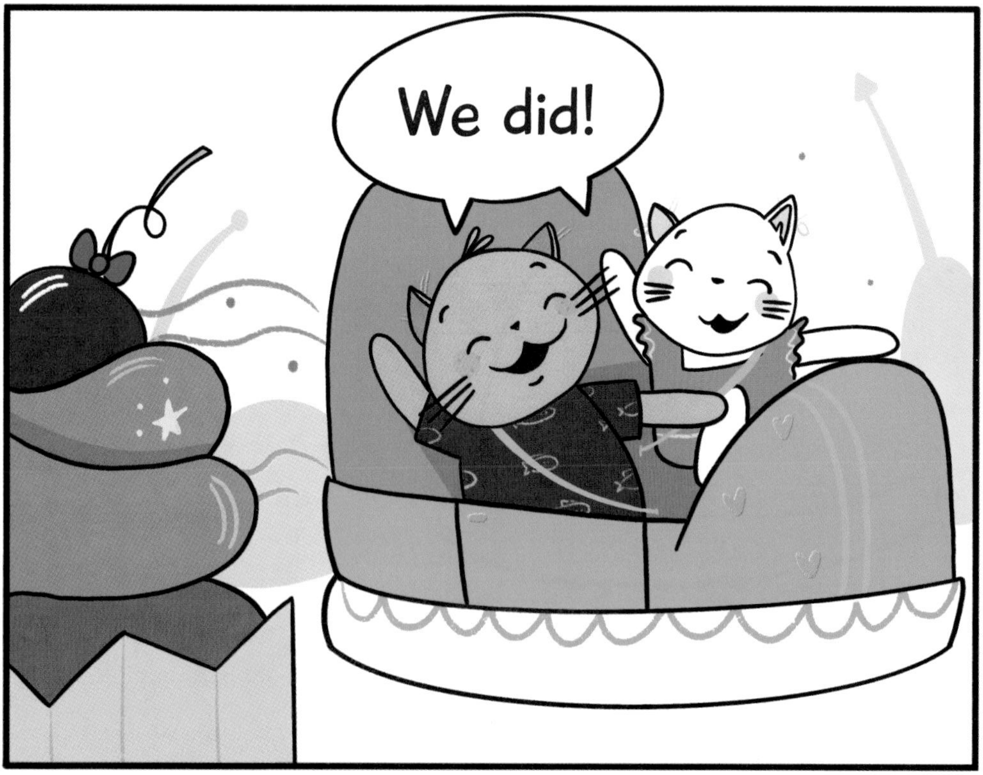
We did!

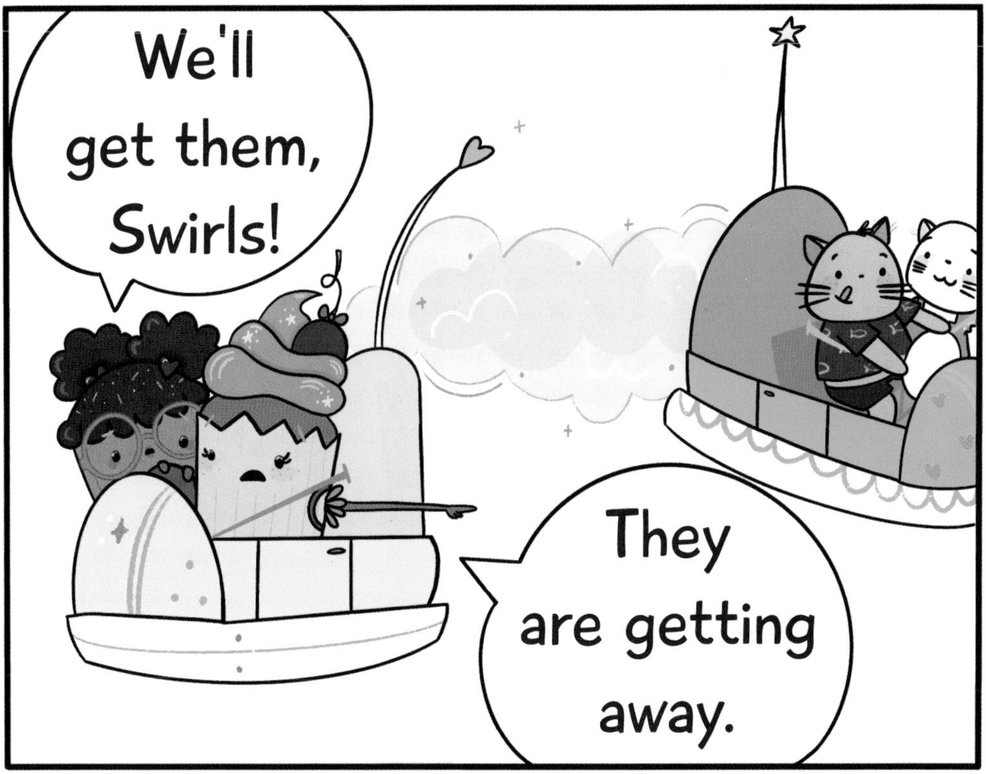
We'll get them, Swirls!
They are getting away.
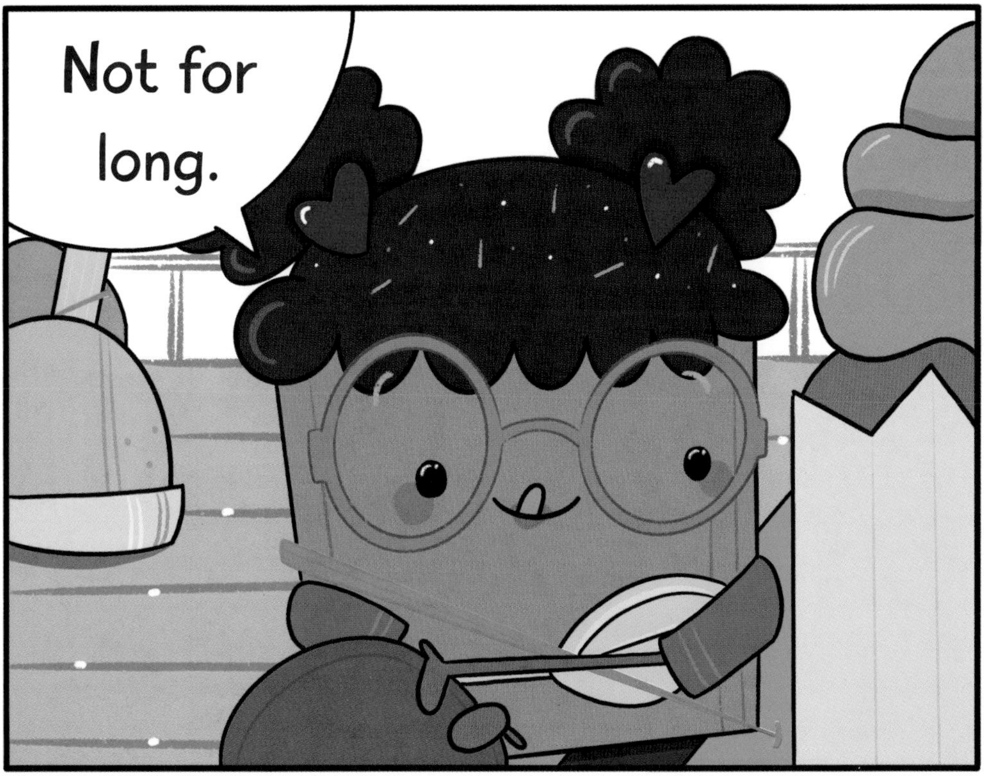
Not for long.

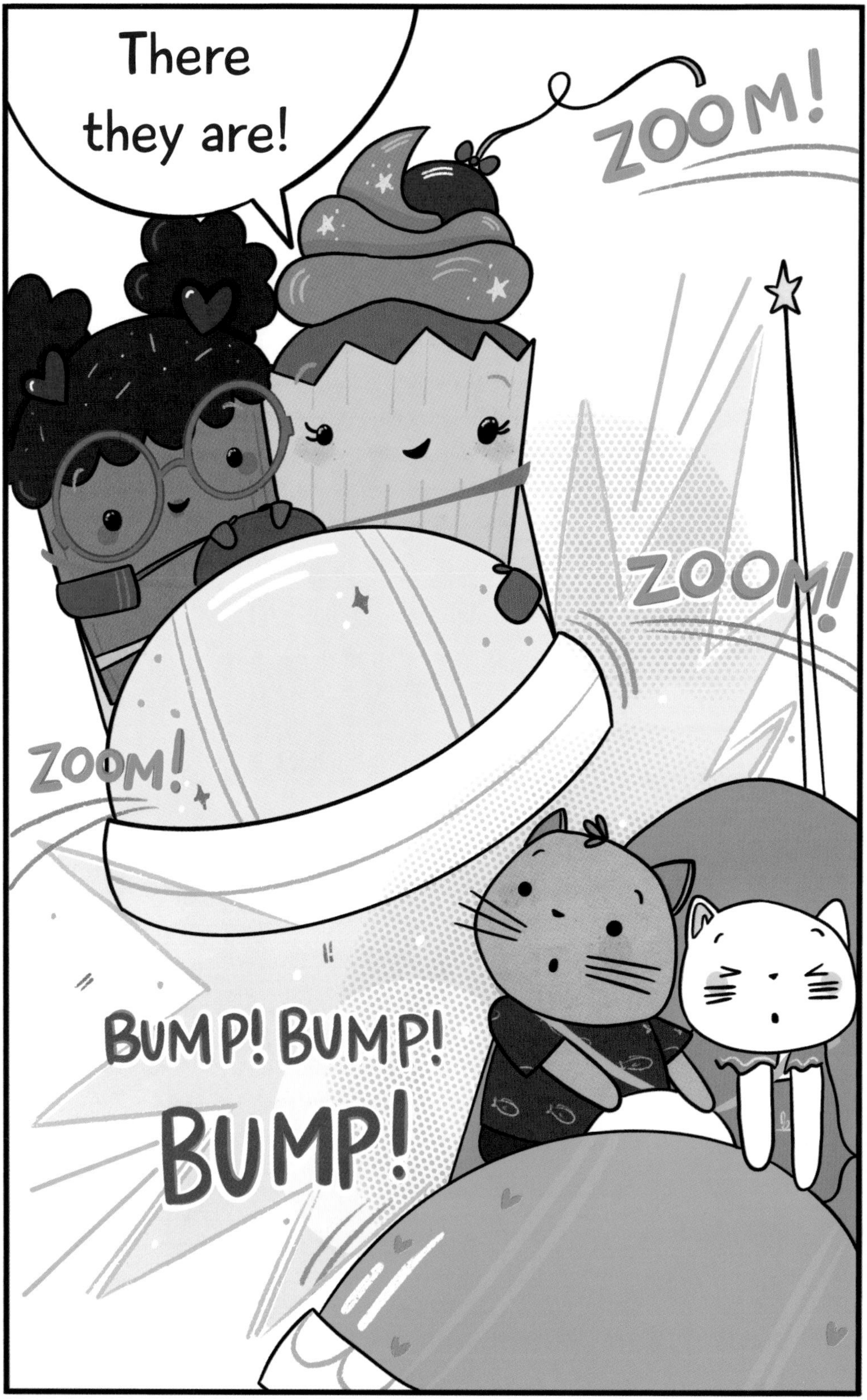
There they are!
ZOOM!
ZOOM!
ZOOM!
BUMP! BUMP!
BUMP!

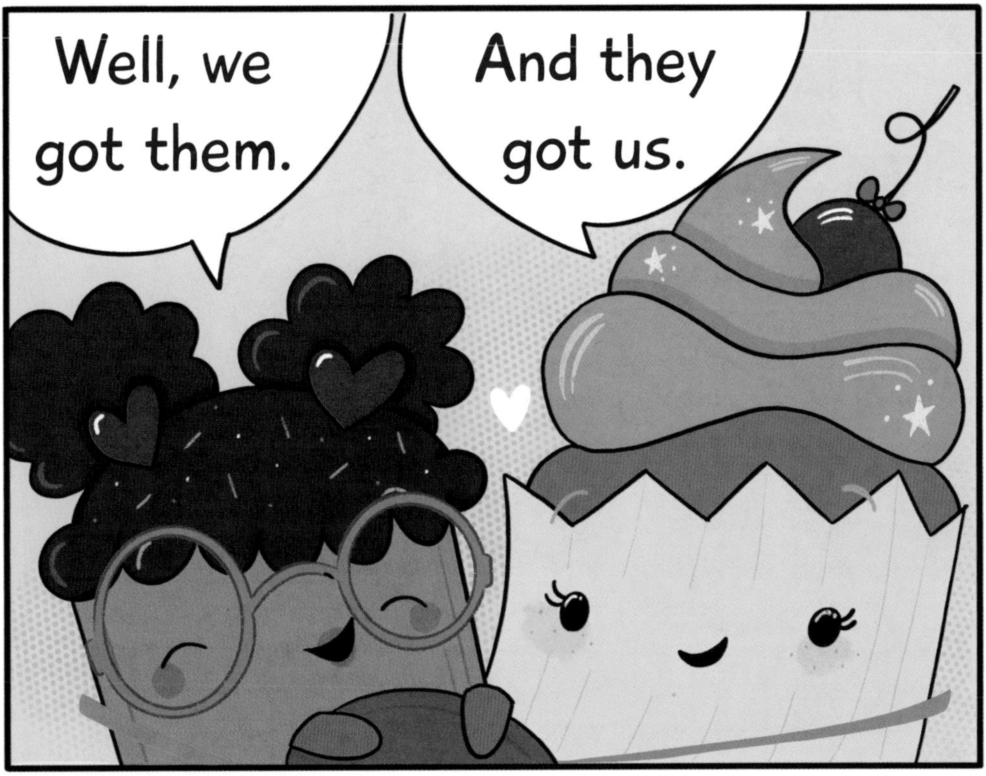
Well, we got them.
And they got us.
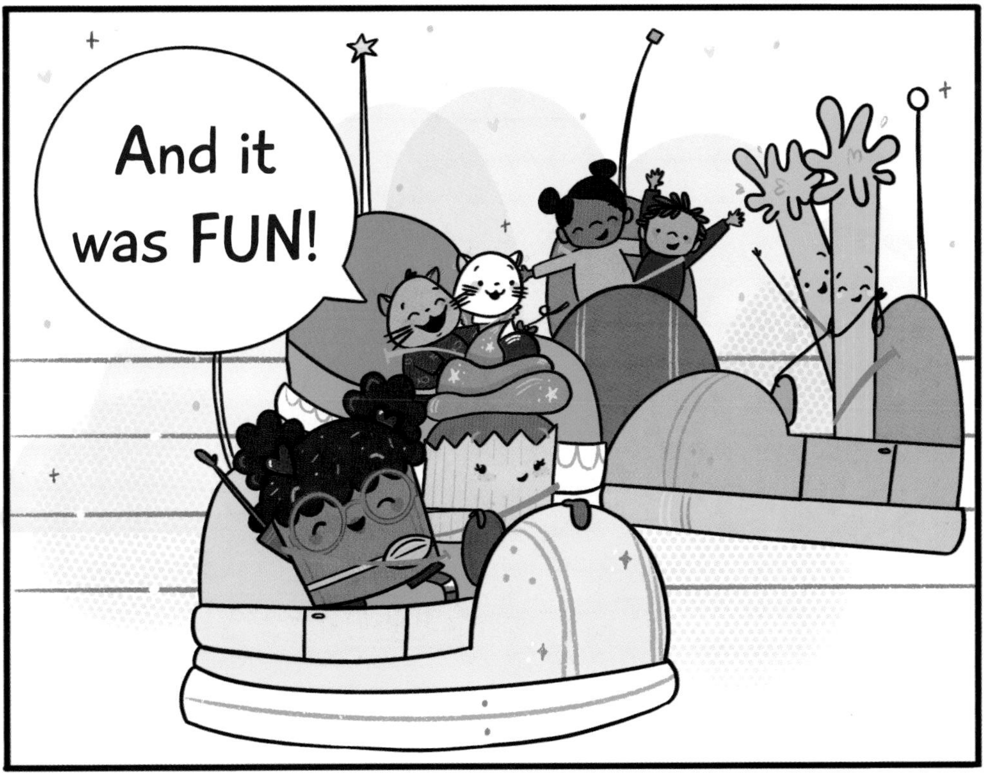
And it was FUN!

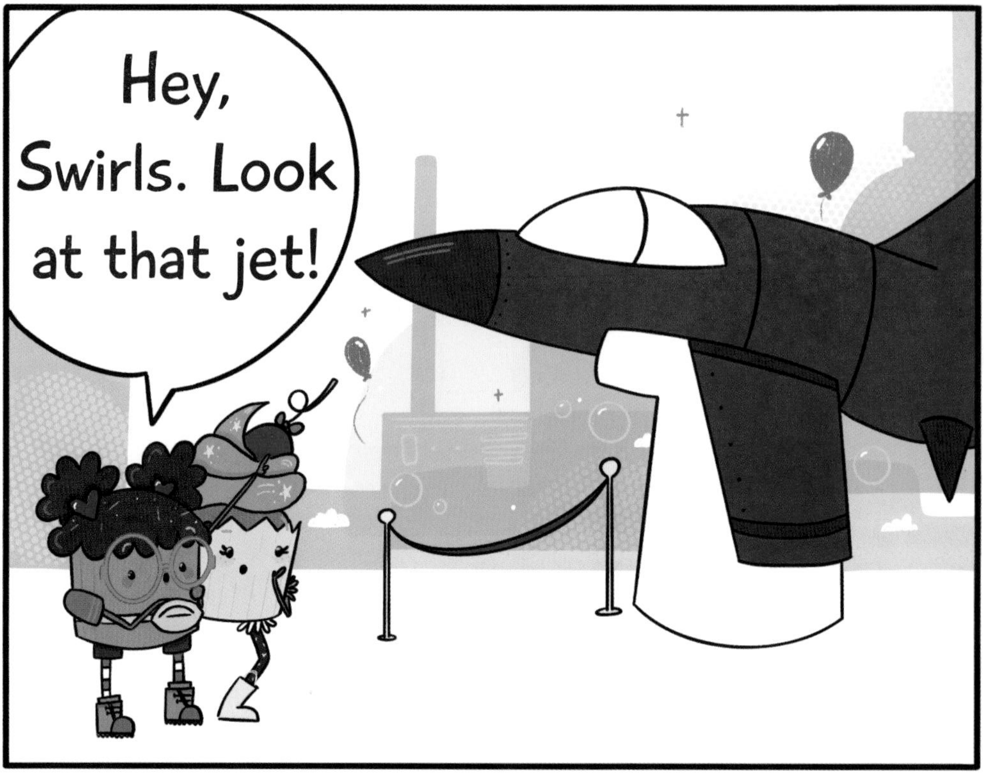
Hey, Swirls. Look at that jet!

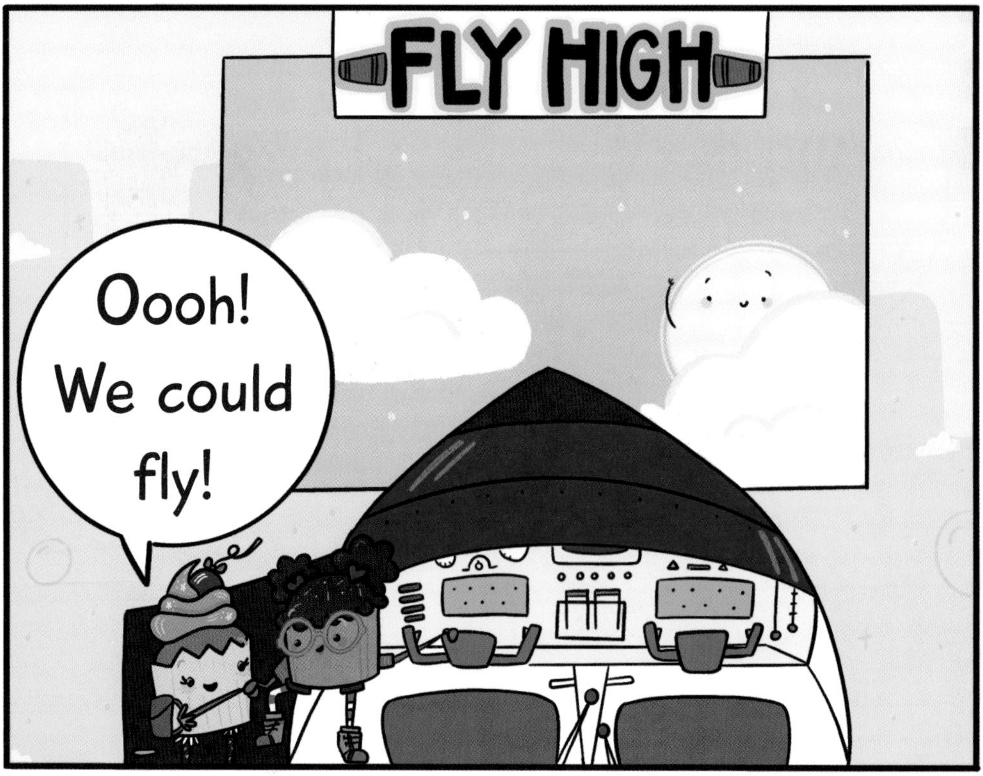
FLY HIGH
Oooh! We could fly!

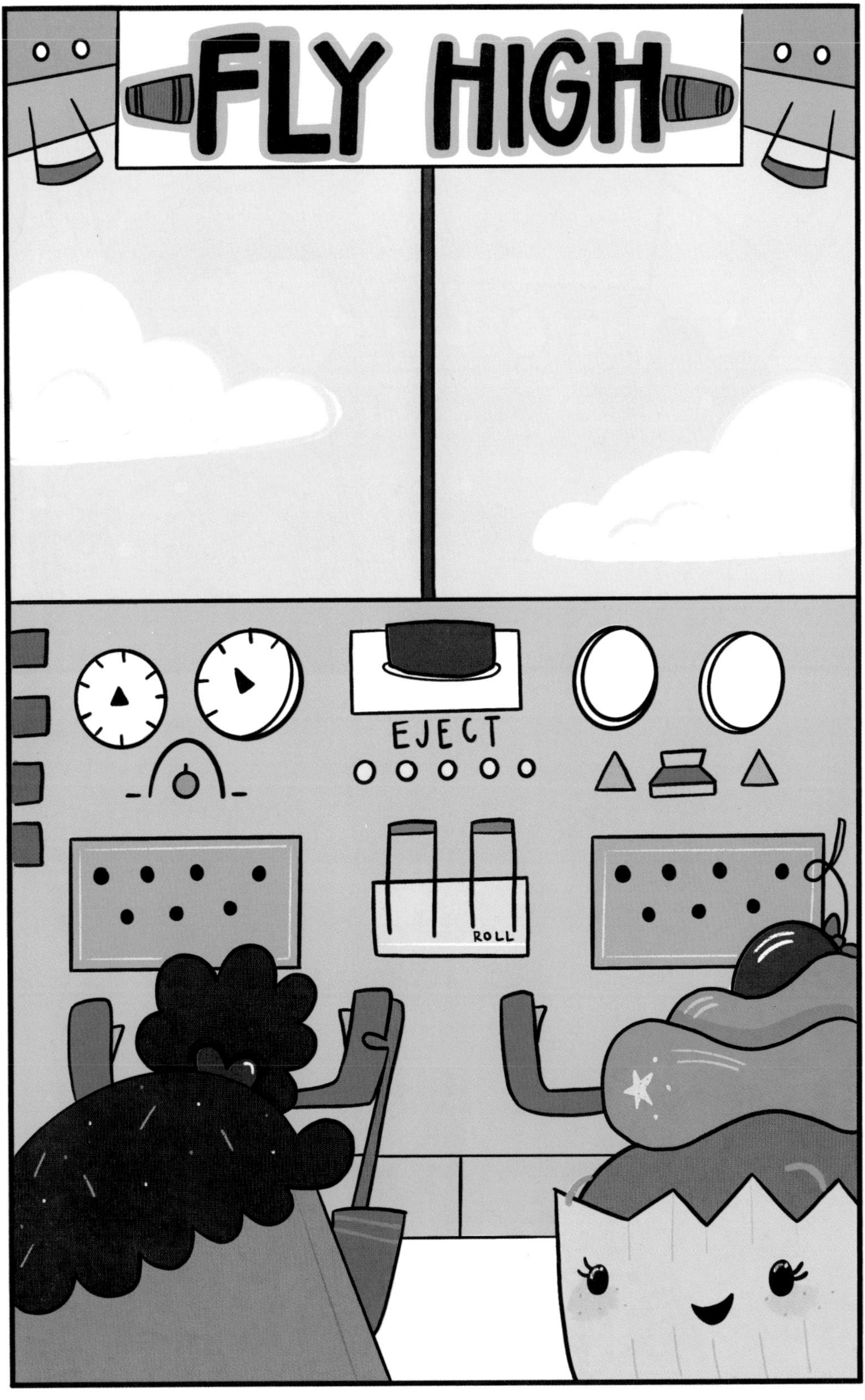
FLY HIGH
EJECT
ROLL

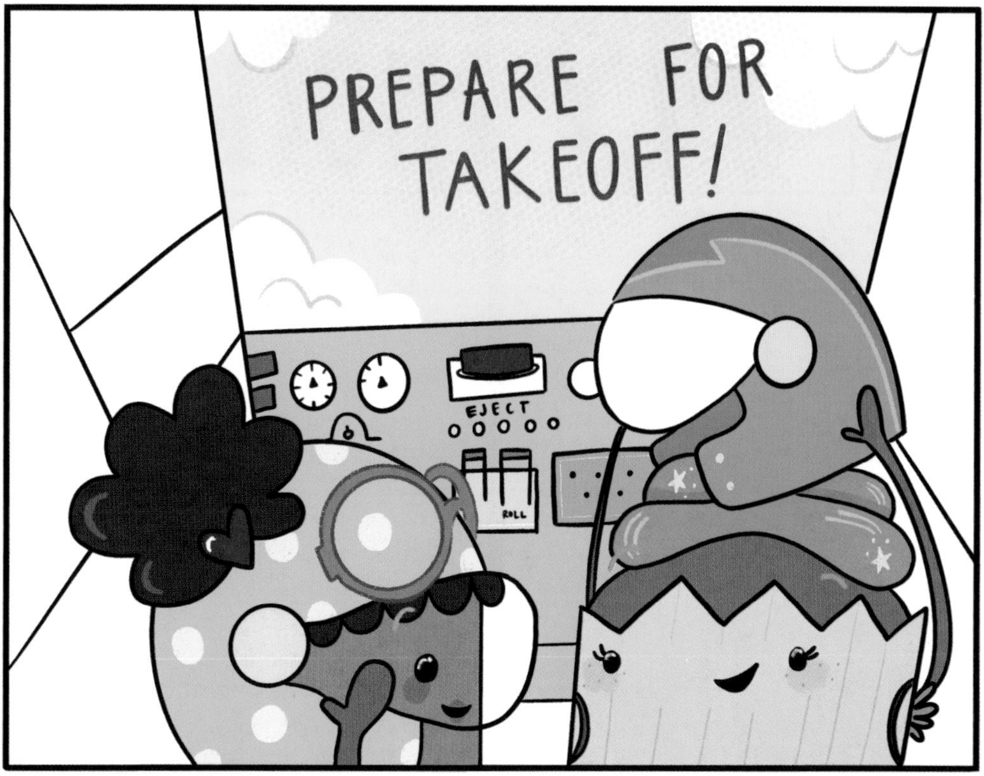
PREPARE FOR TAKEOFF!
EJECT
ROLL

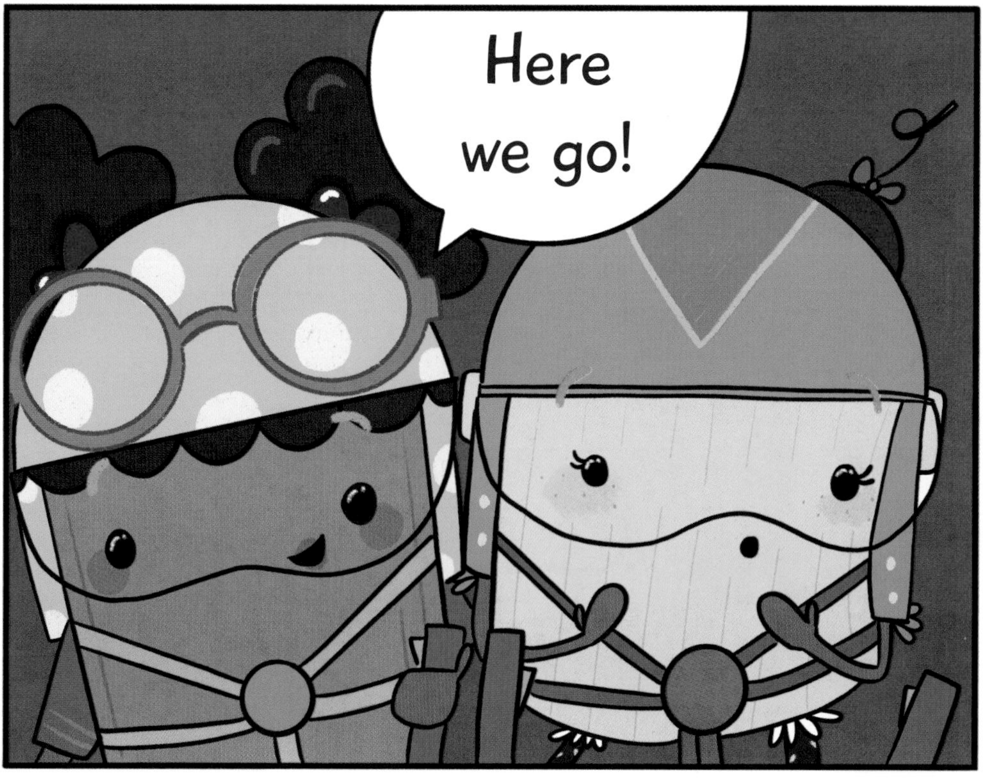
Here we go!

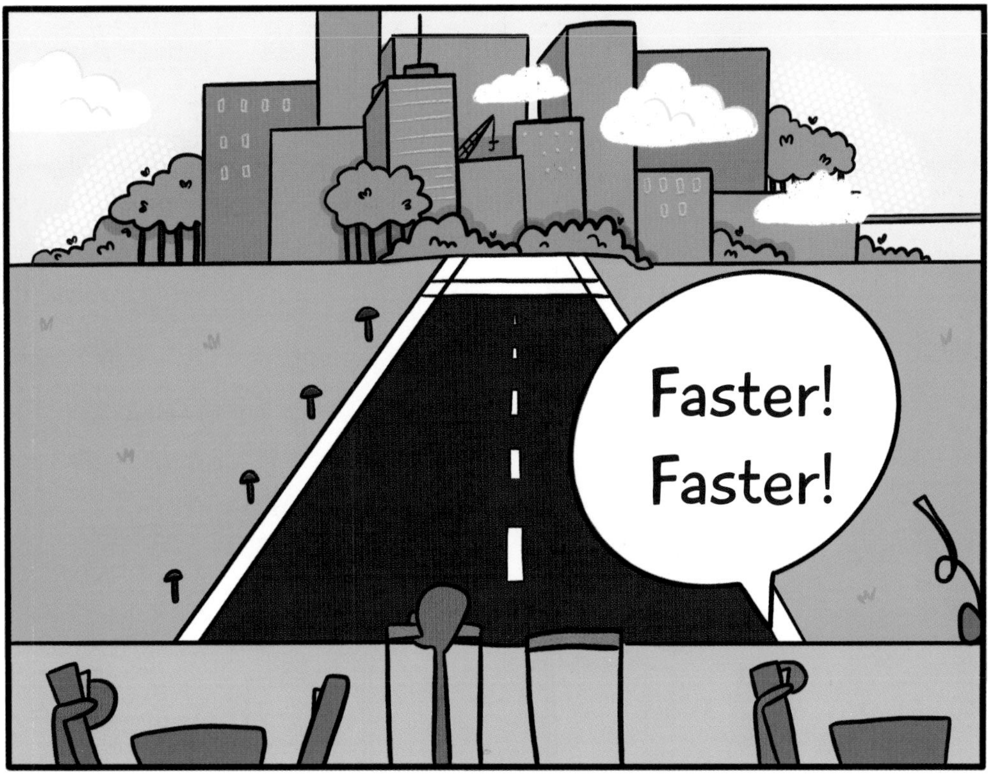
Faster! Faster!

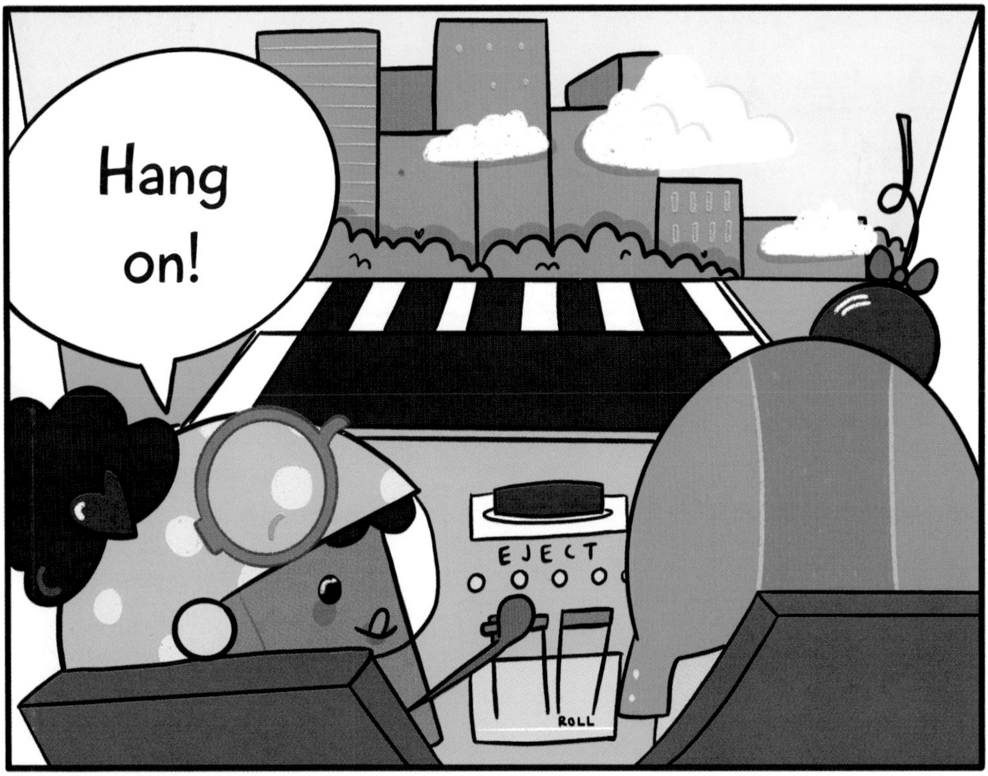
Hang on!
EJECT
ROLL

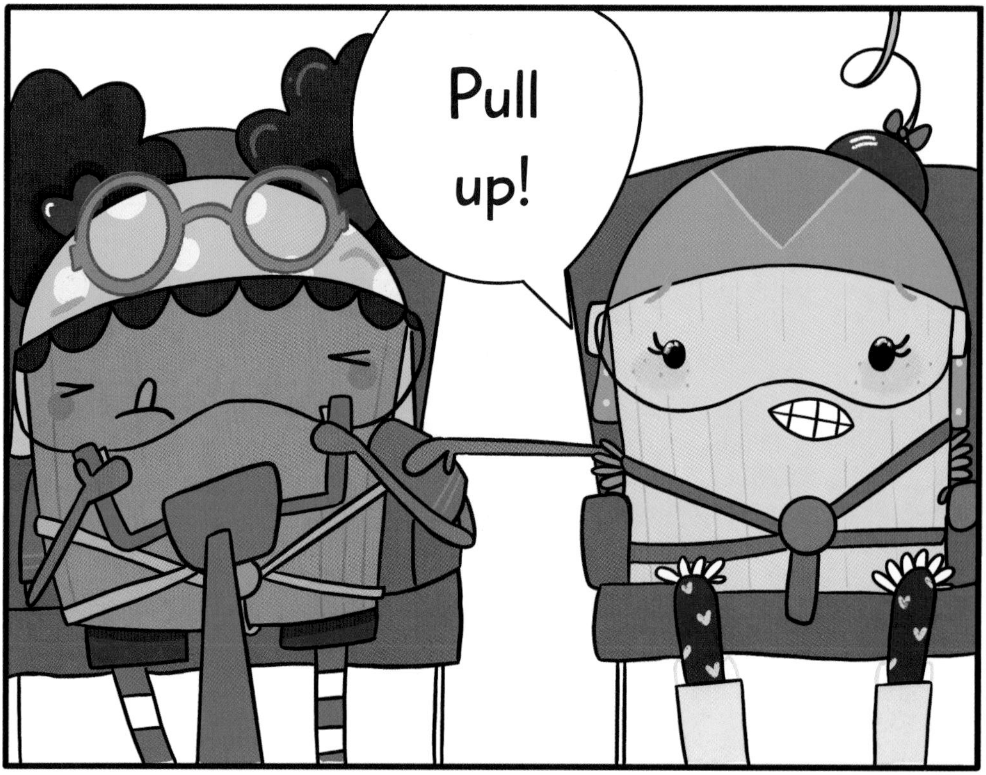
Pull up!

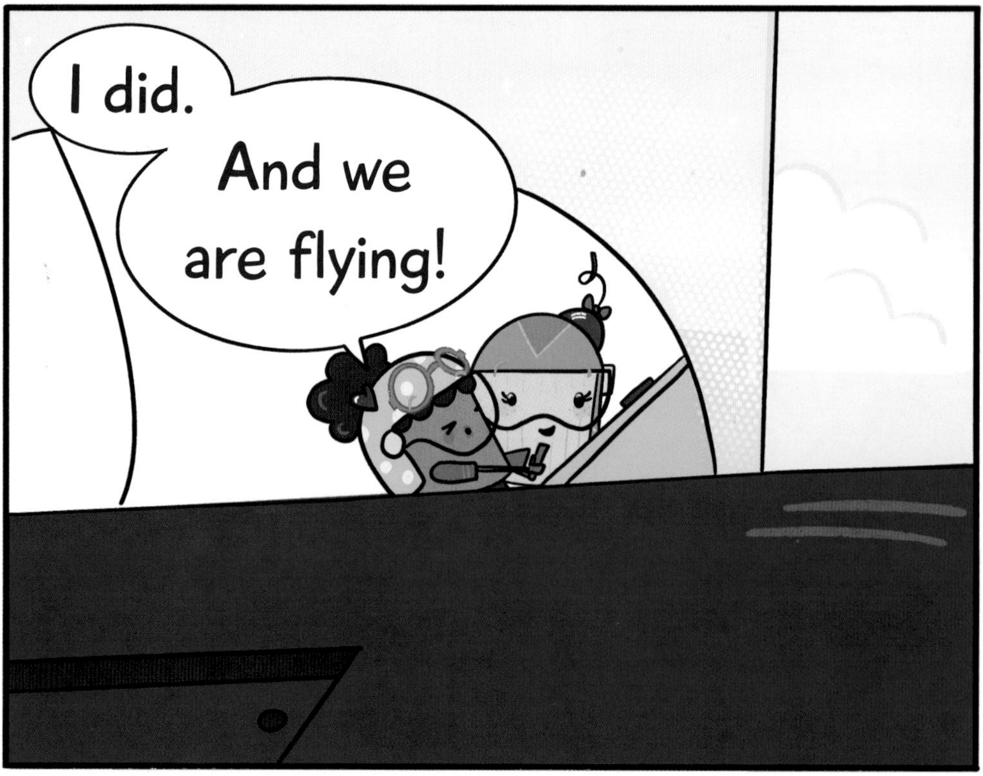
I did.
And we are flying!

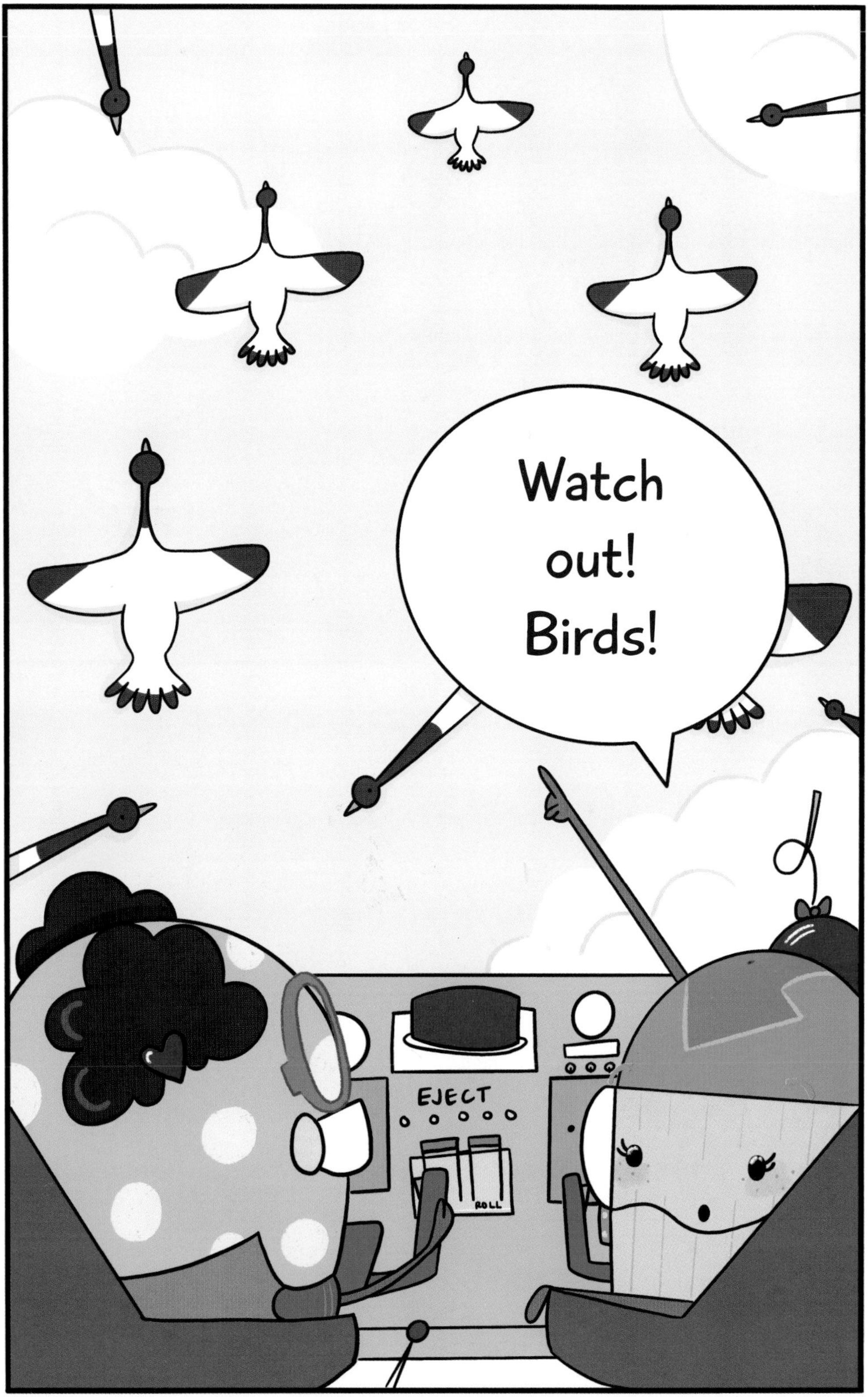
Watch out! Birds!
EJECT
ROLL

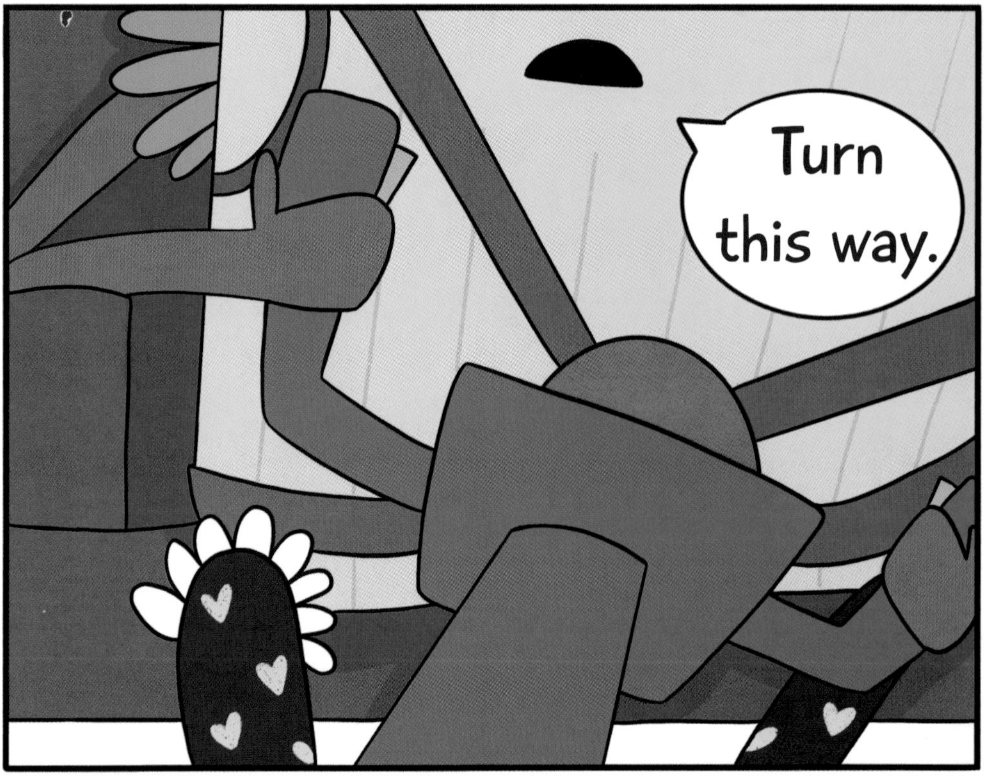
Turn this way.

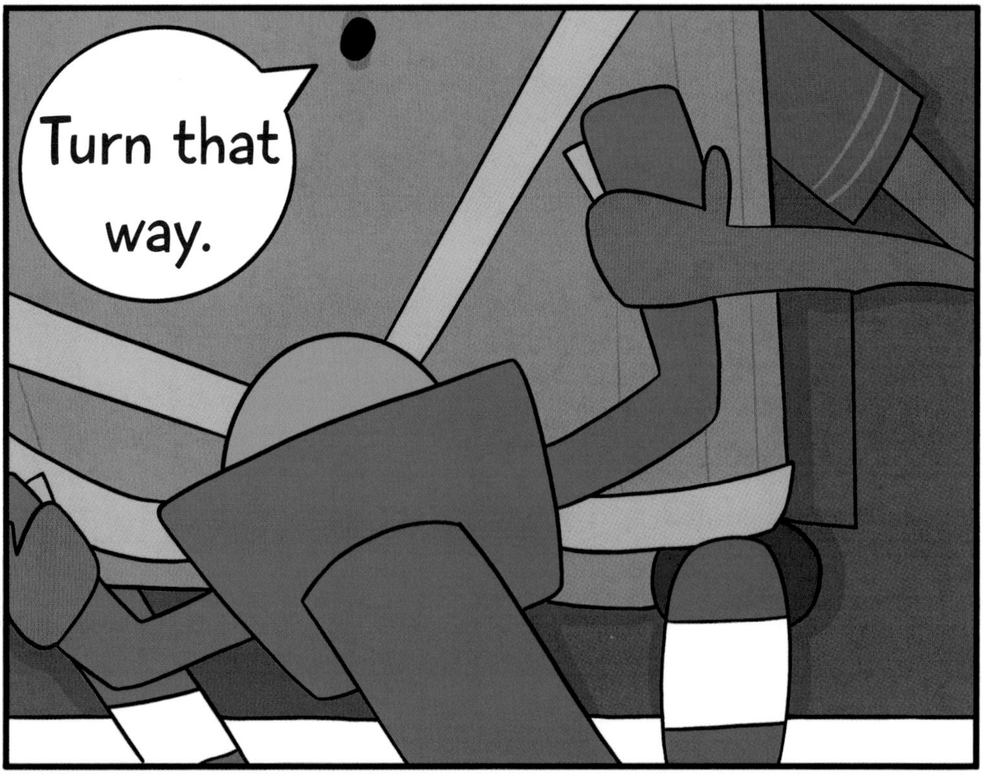
Turn that way.

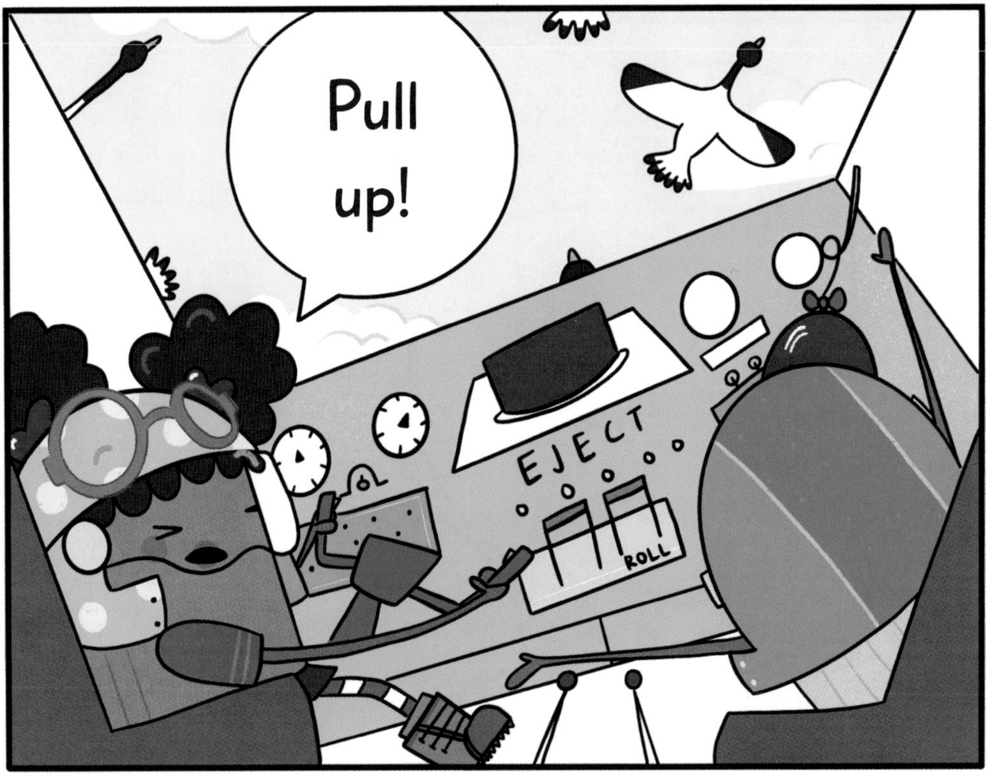
Pull up!
EJECT
ROLL

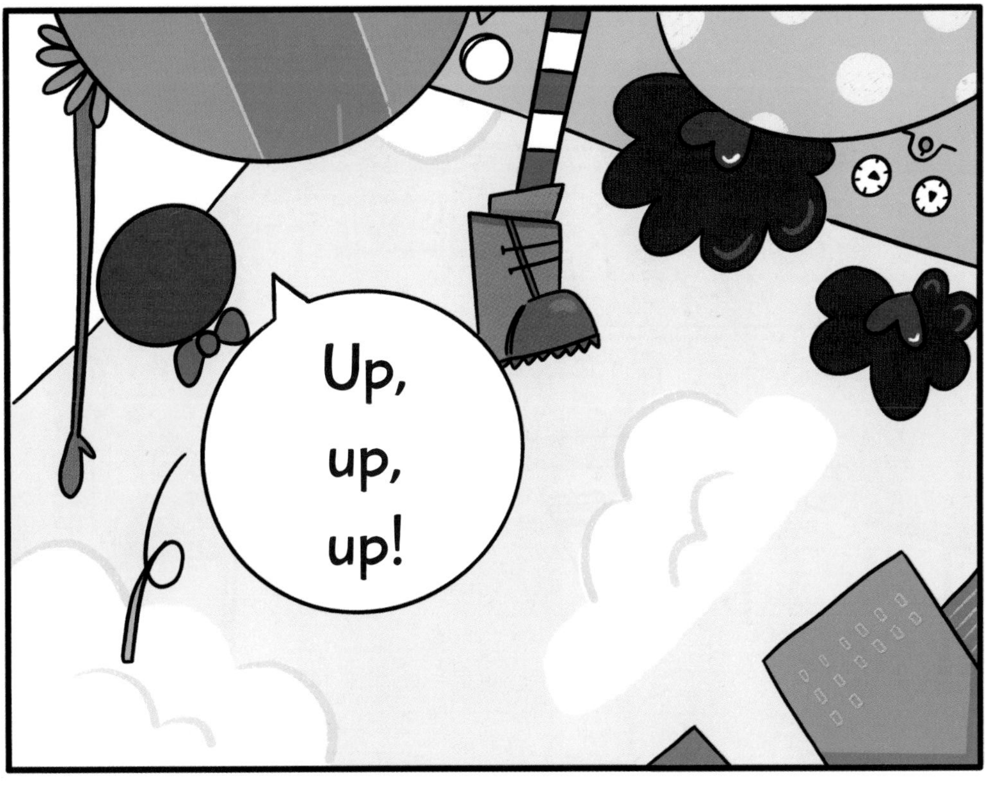
Up, up, up!

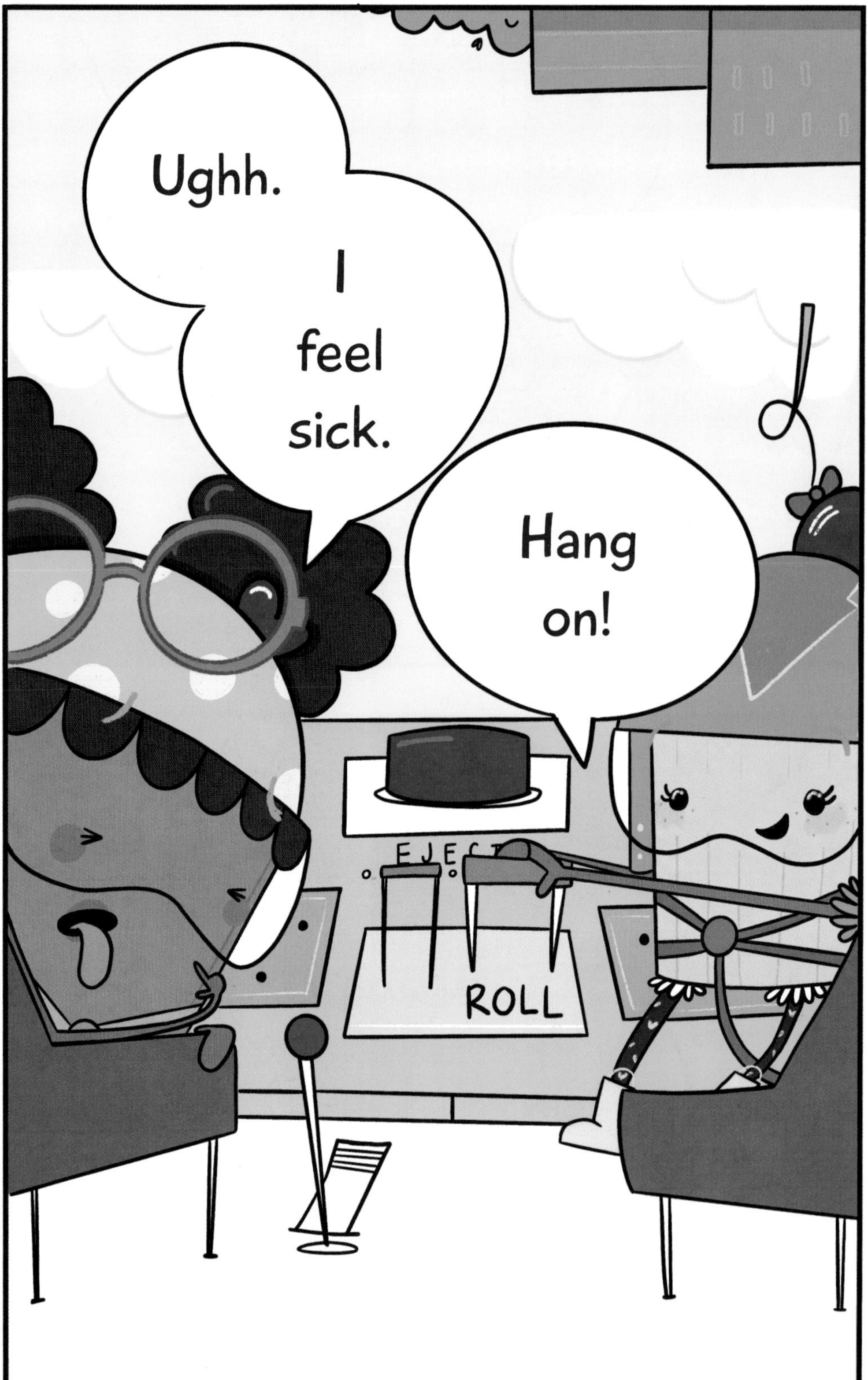
Ughh.
I feel sick.
Hang on!
EJECT
ROLL

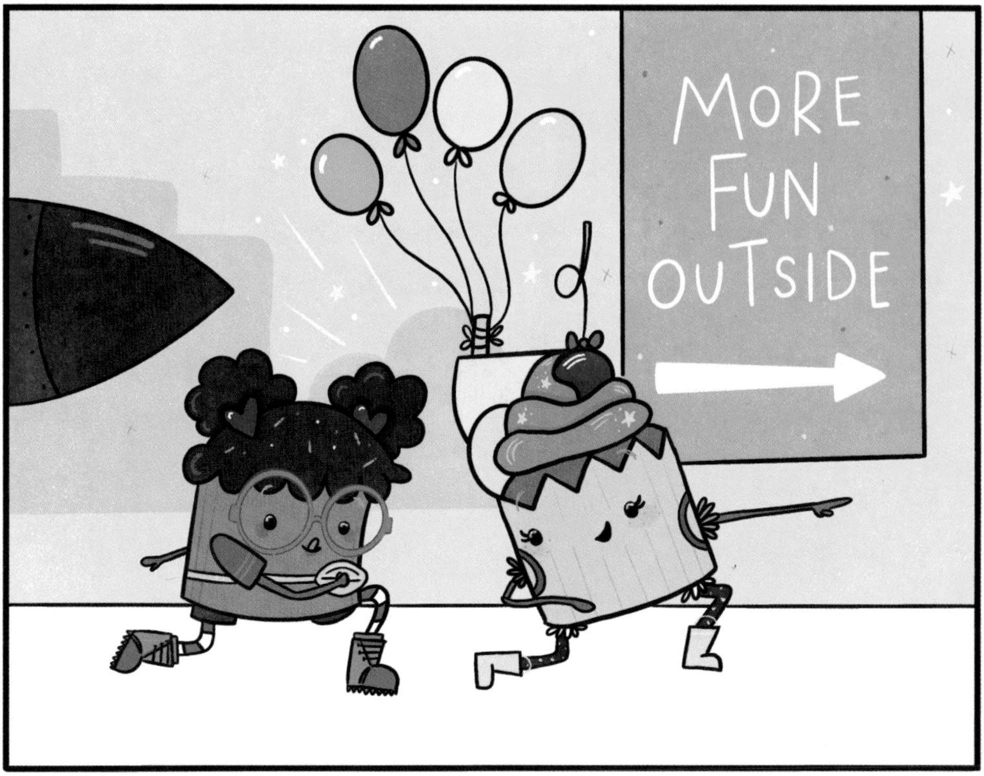
MORE FUN OUTSIDE

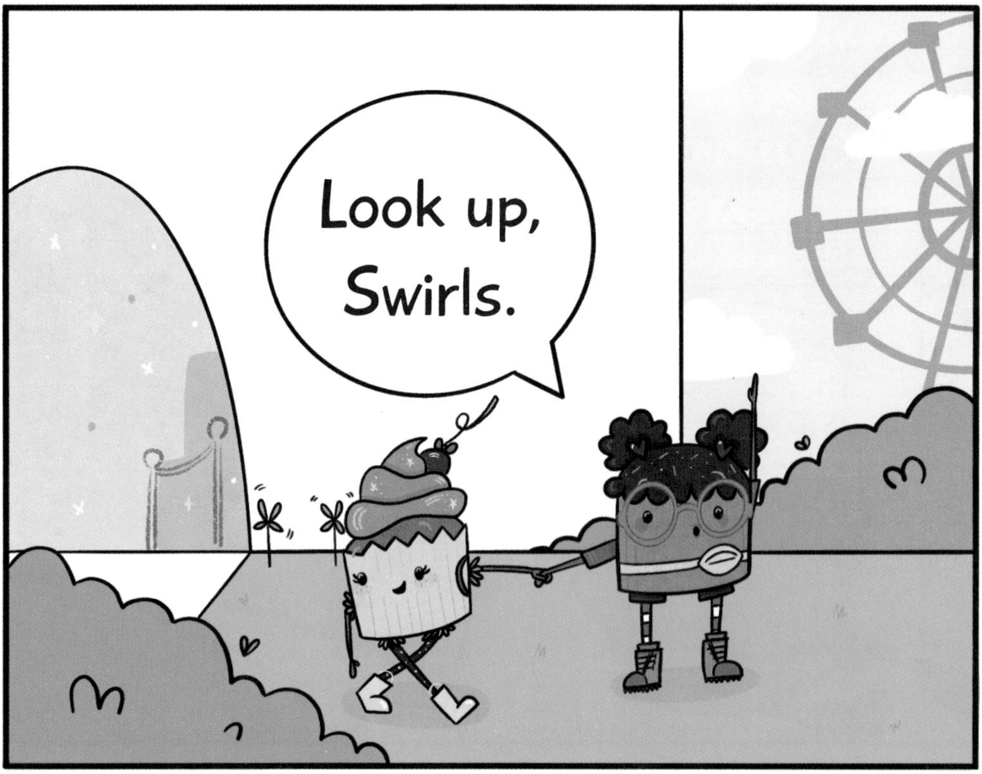
Look up, Swirls.

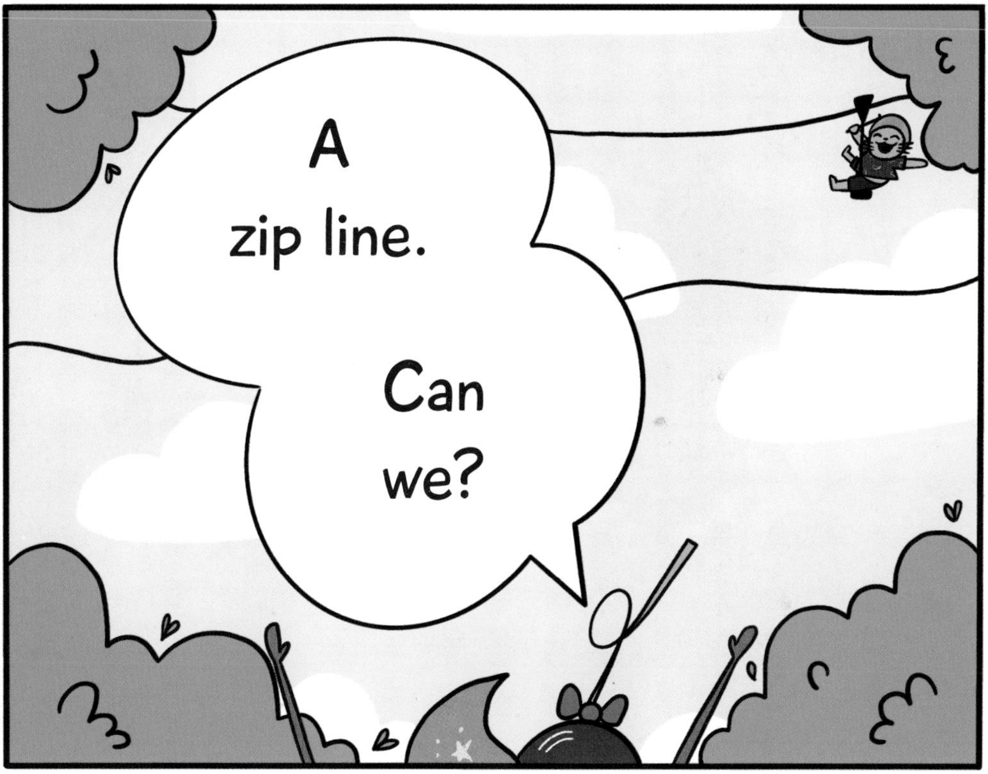
A zip line.
Can we?

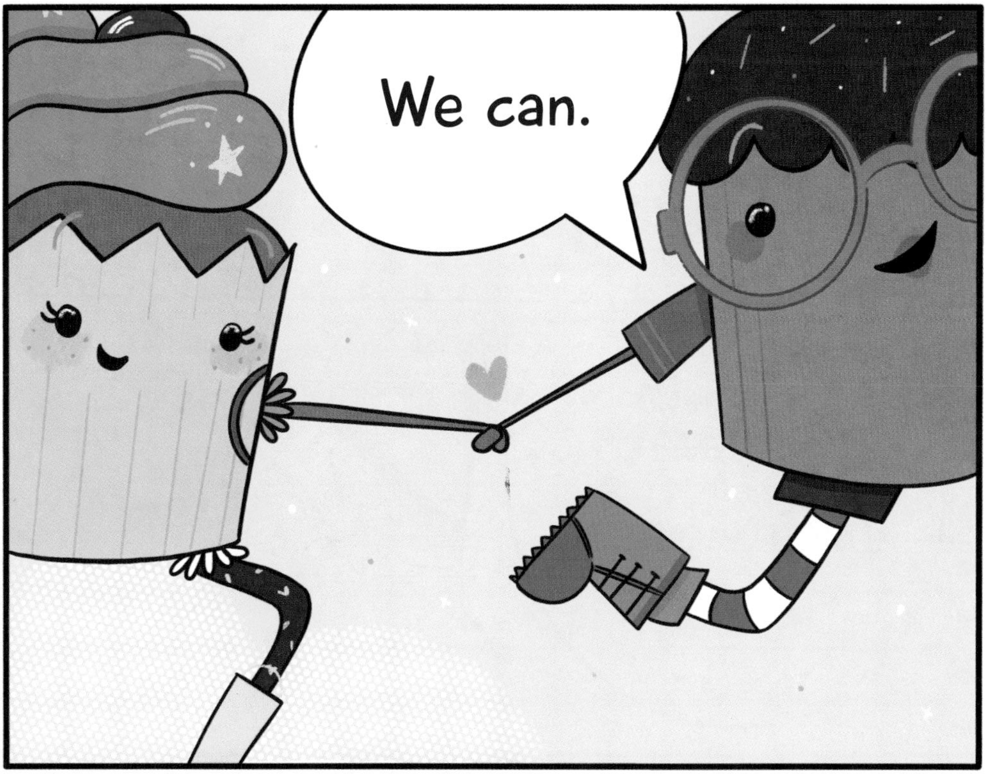
We can.

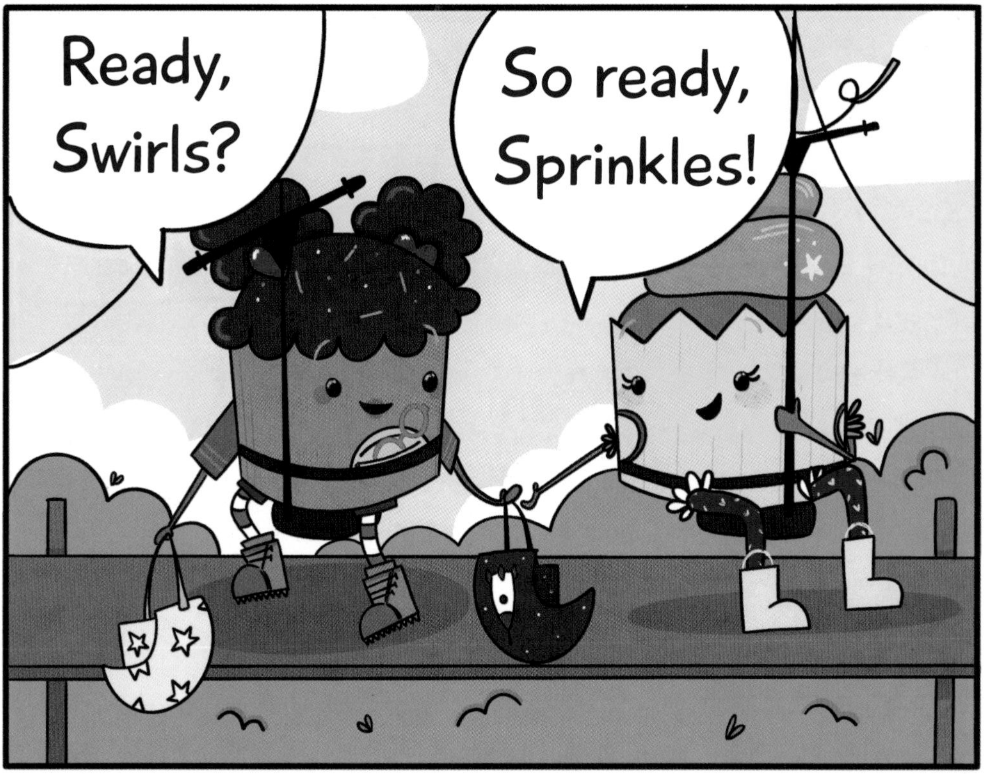
Ready, Swirls?
So ready, Sprinkles!

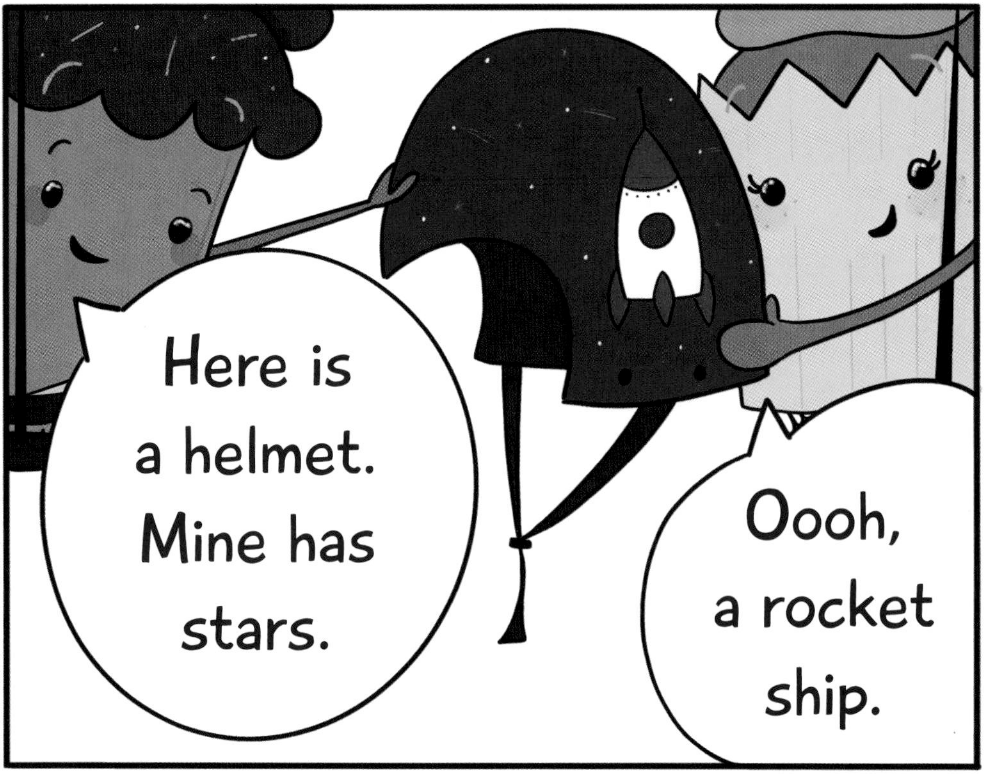
Here is a helmet. Mine has stars.
Oooh, a rocket ship.

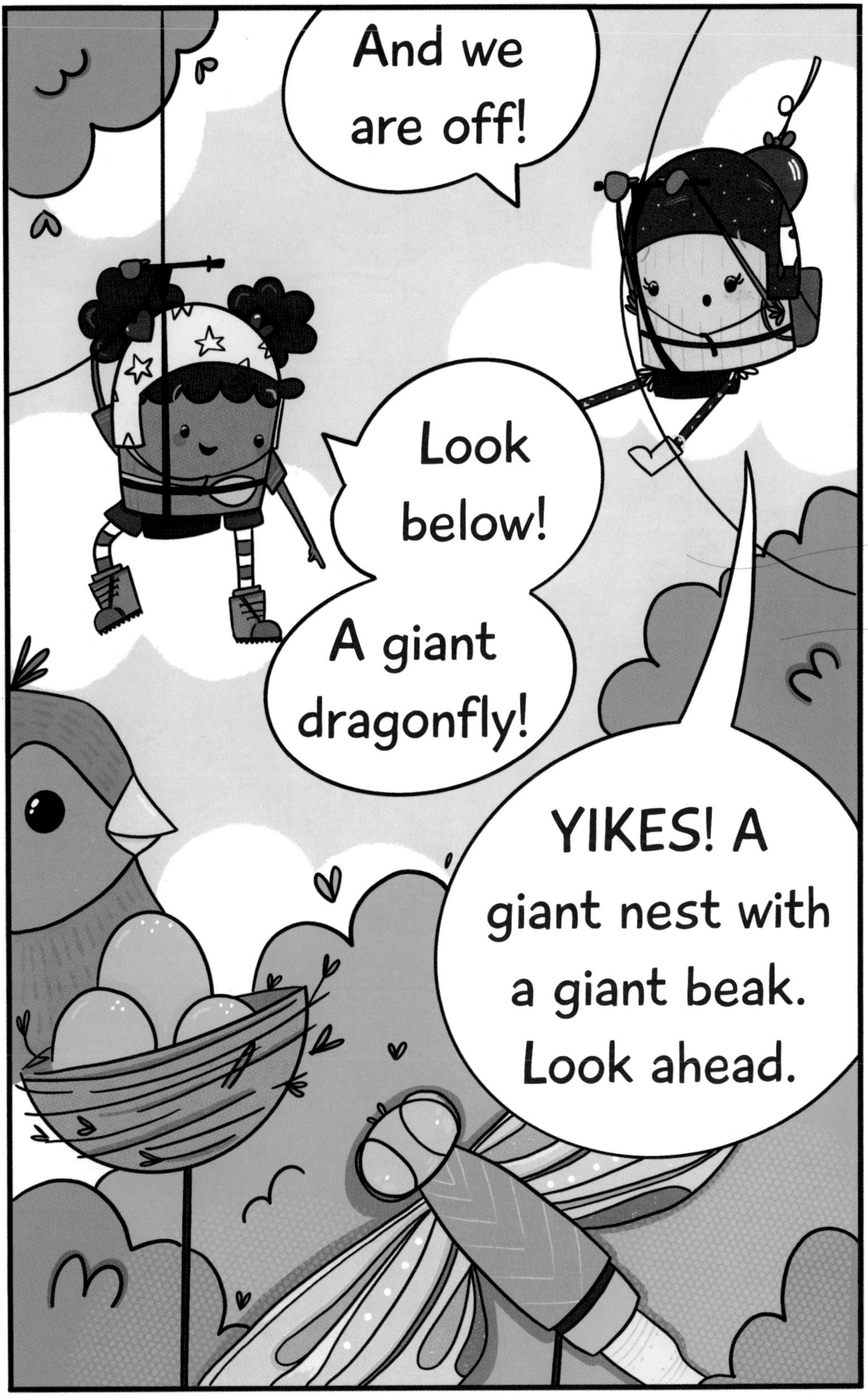
And we are off!
Look below!
A giant dragonfly!
YIKES! A giant nest with a giant beak. Look ahead.

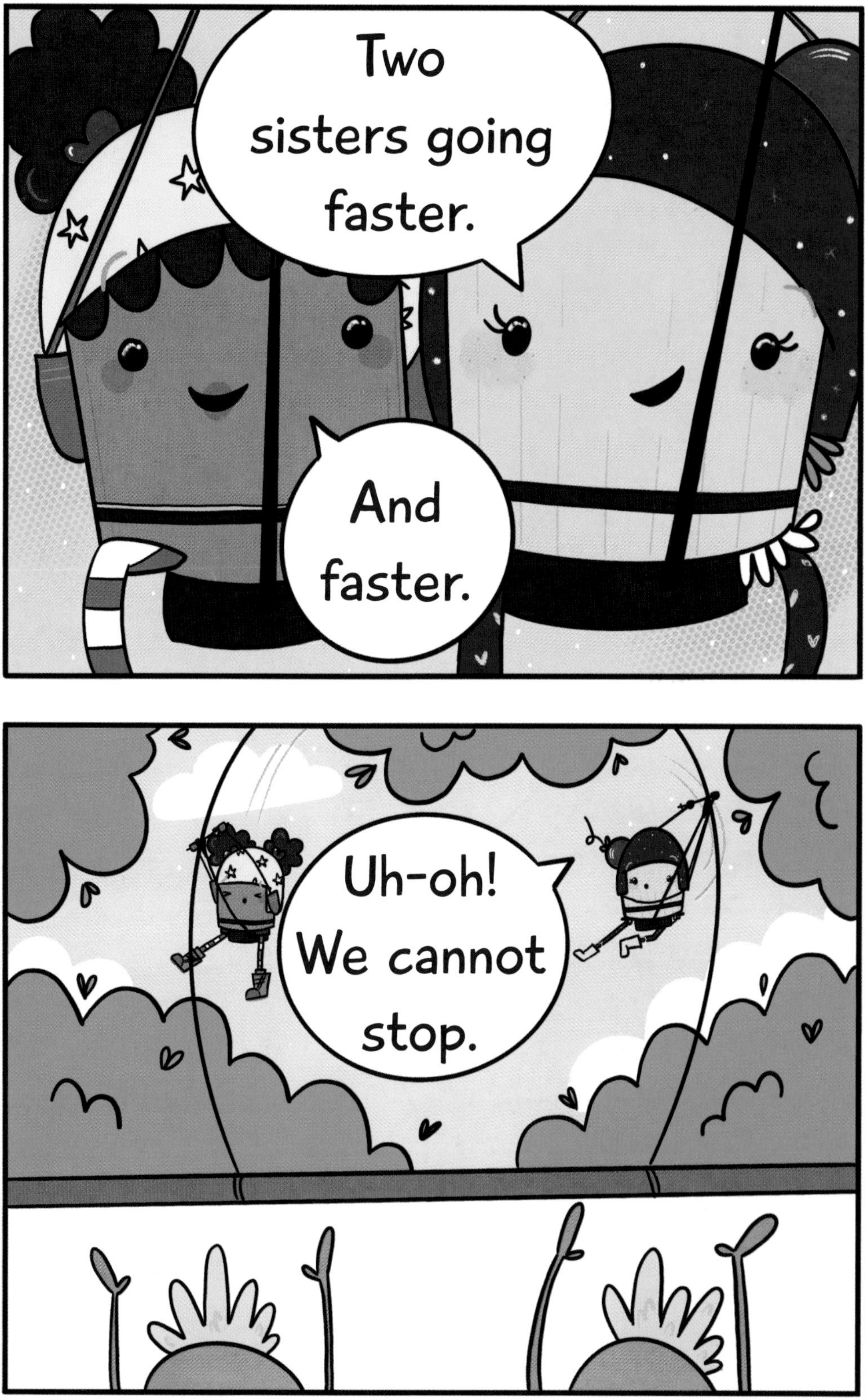
Two sisters going faster.
And faster.
Uh-oh! We cannot stop.

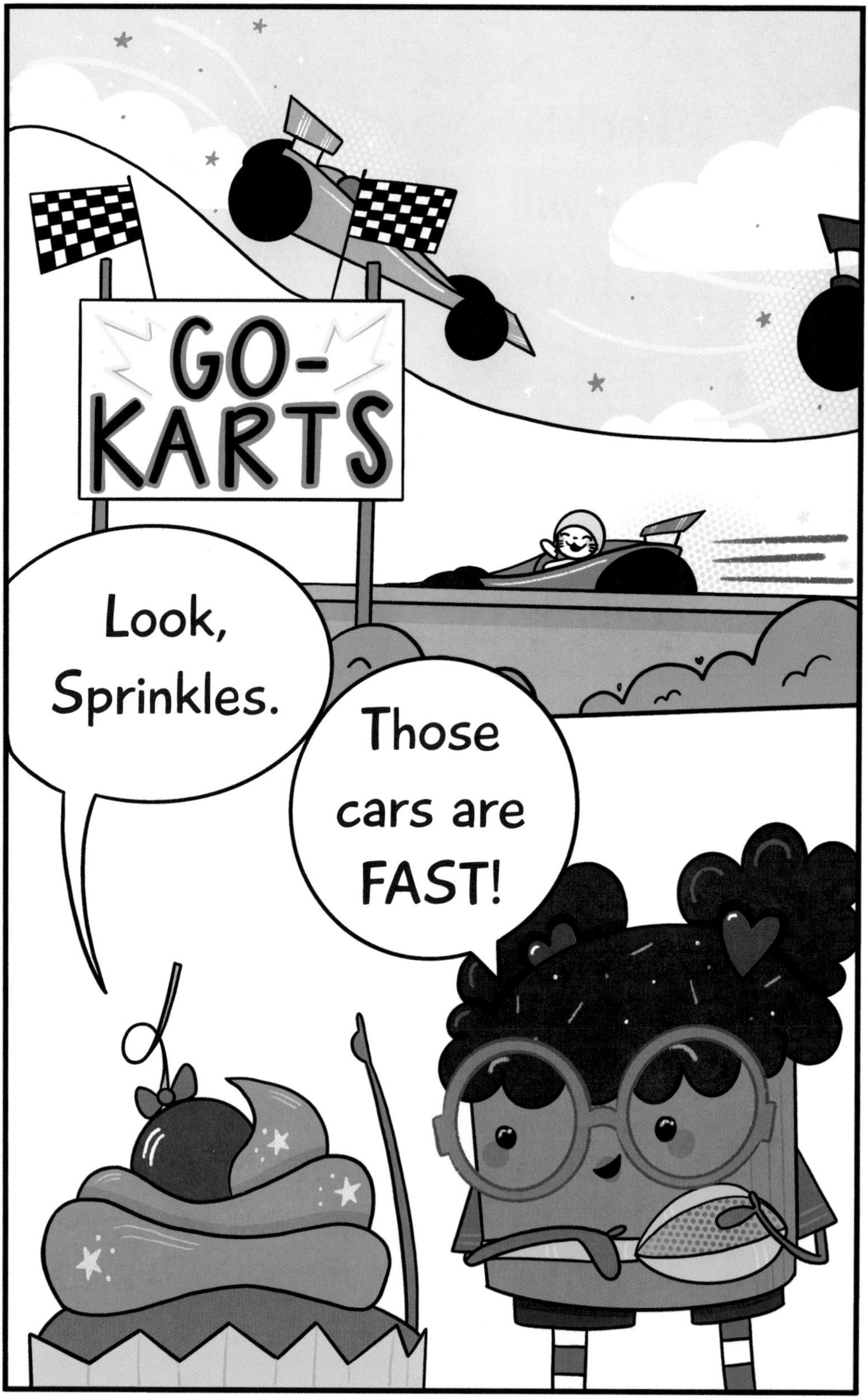
GO-KARTS
Look, Sprinkles.
Those cars are FAST!

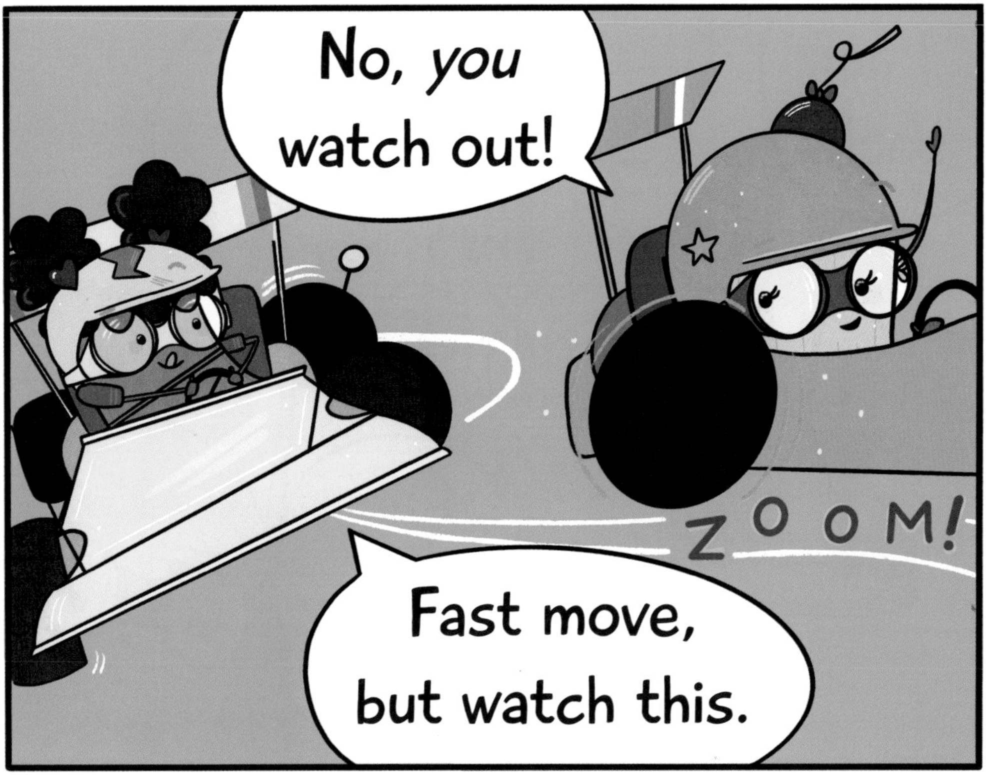
No, *you* watch out!
ZOOM!
Fast move, but watch this.

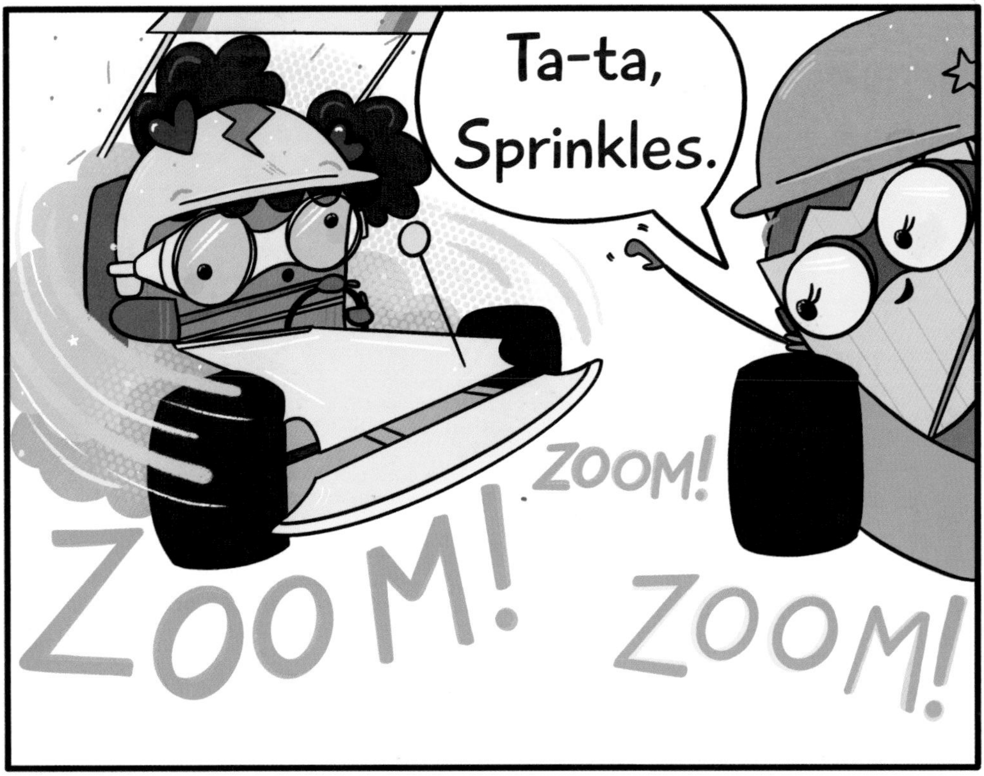
Ta-ta, Sprinkles.
ZOOM!
ZOOM!
ZOOM!

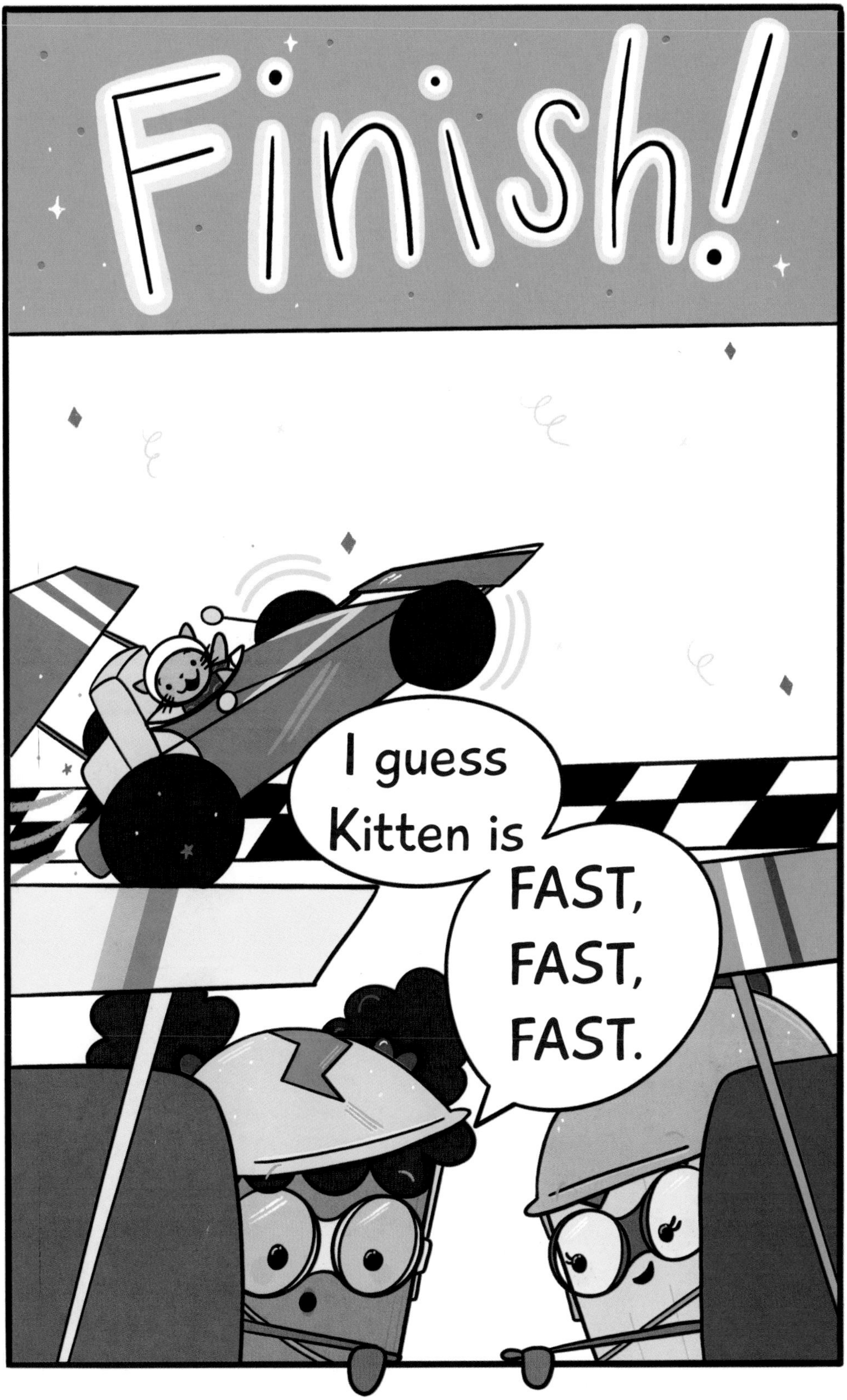
Finish!
I guess Kitten is
FAST, FAST, FAST.

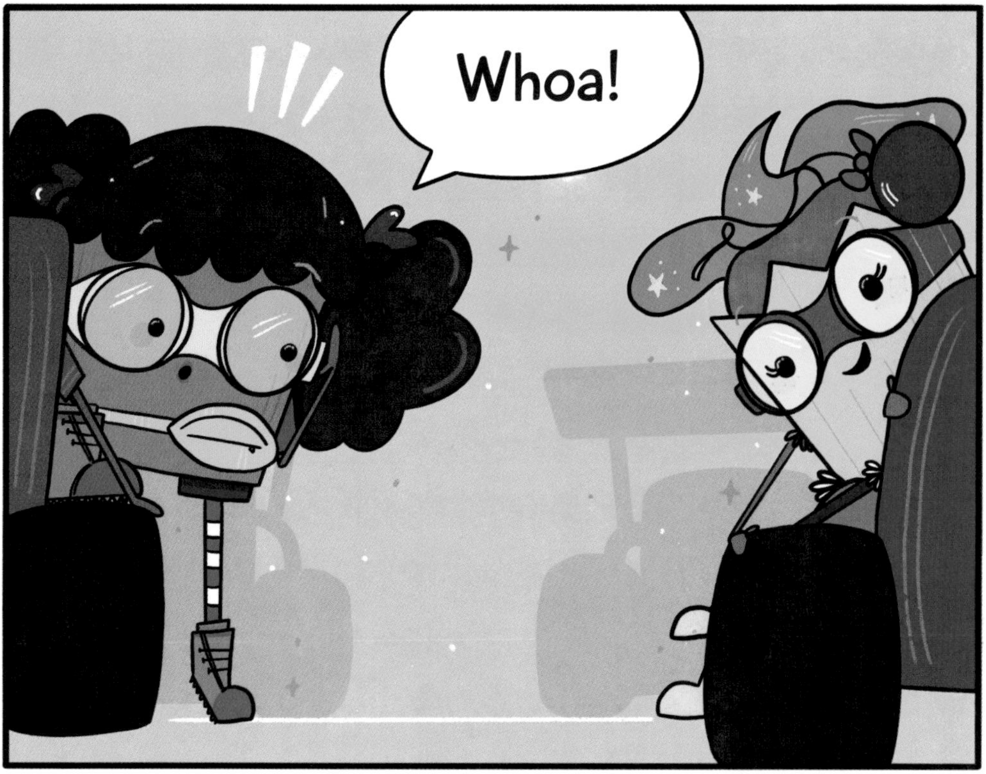
Whoa!

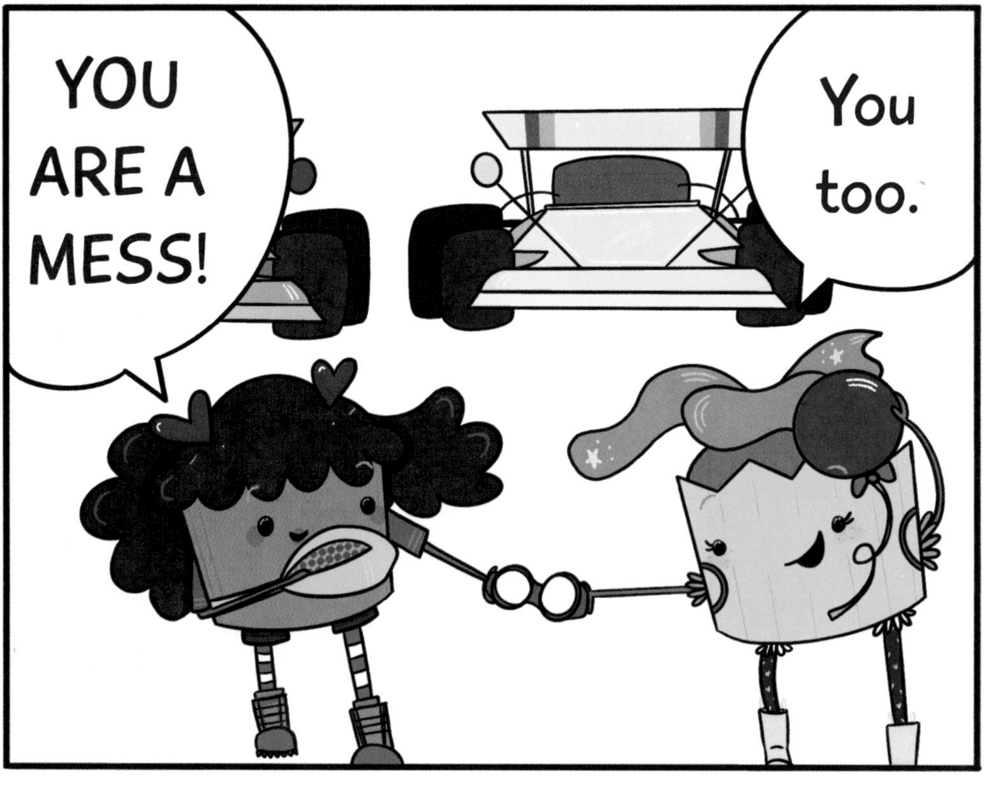
YOU ARE A MESS!
You too.

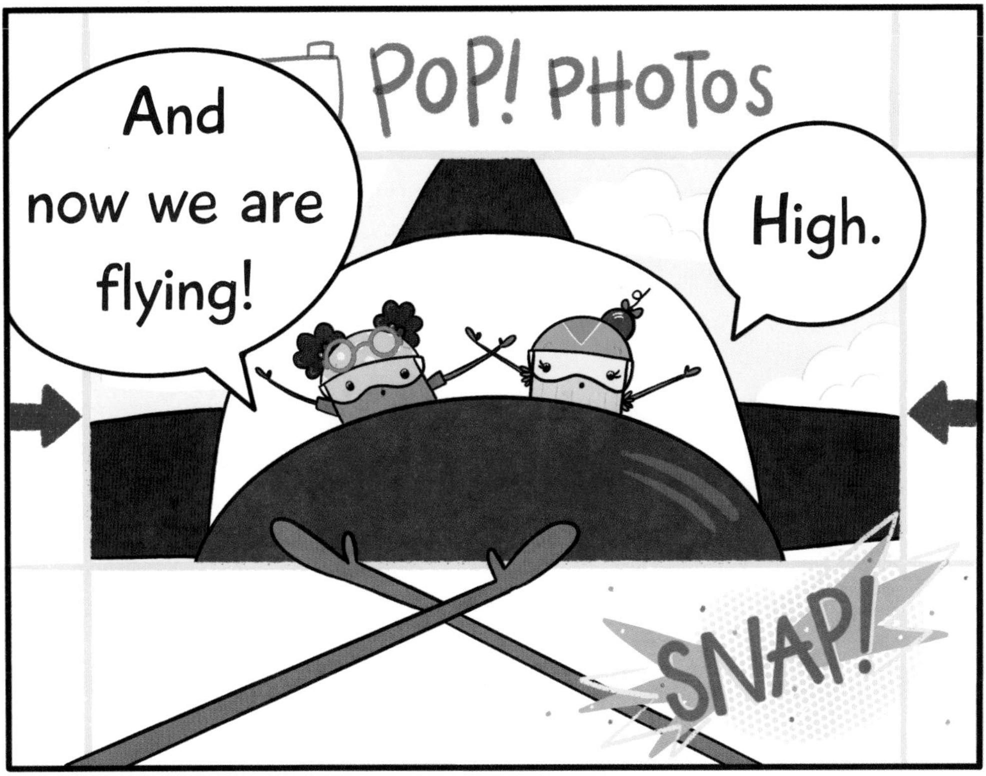
POP! PHOTOS
And now we are flying!
High.
SNAP!

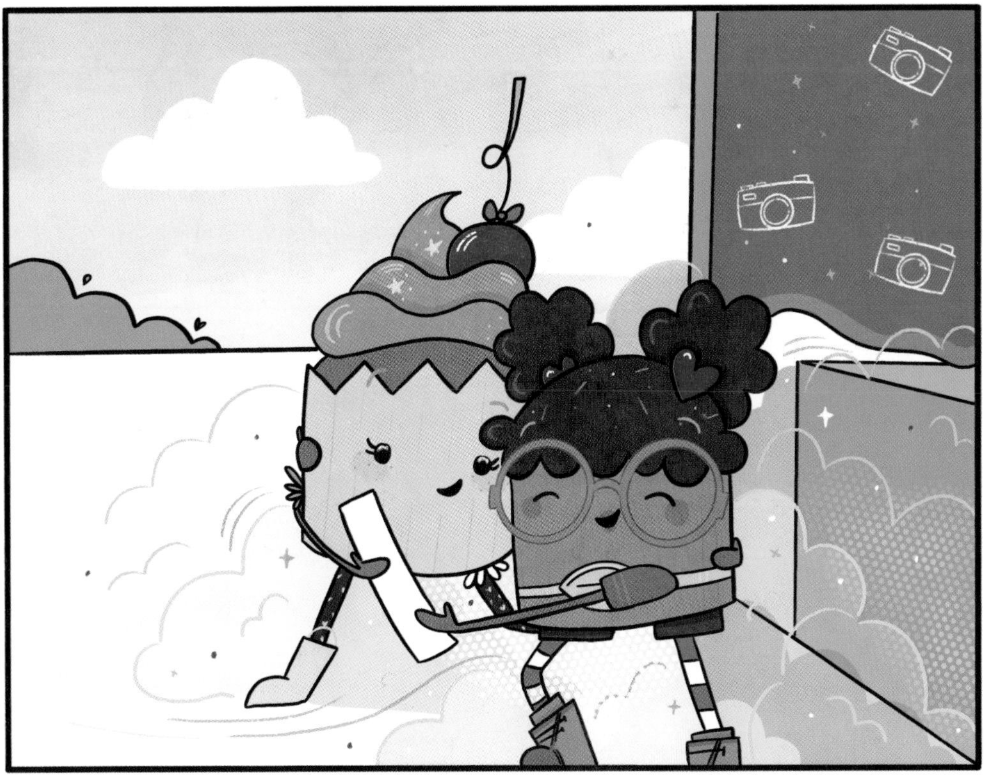

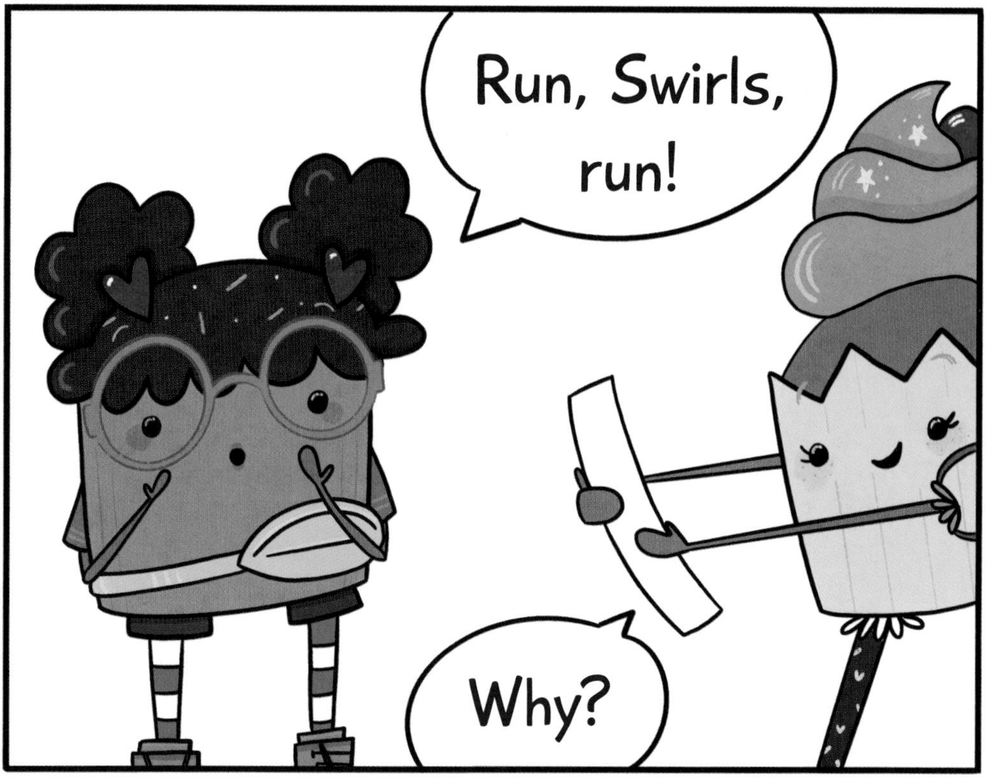
Run, Swirls,
run!
Why?
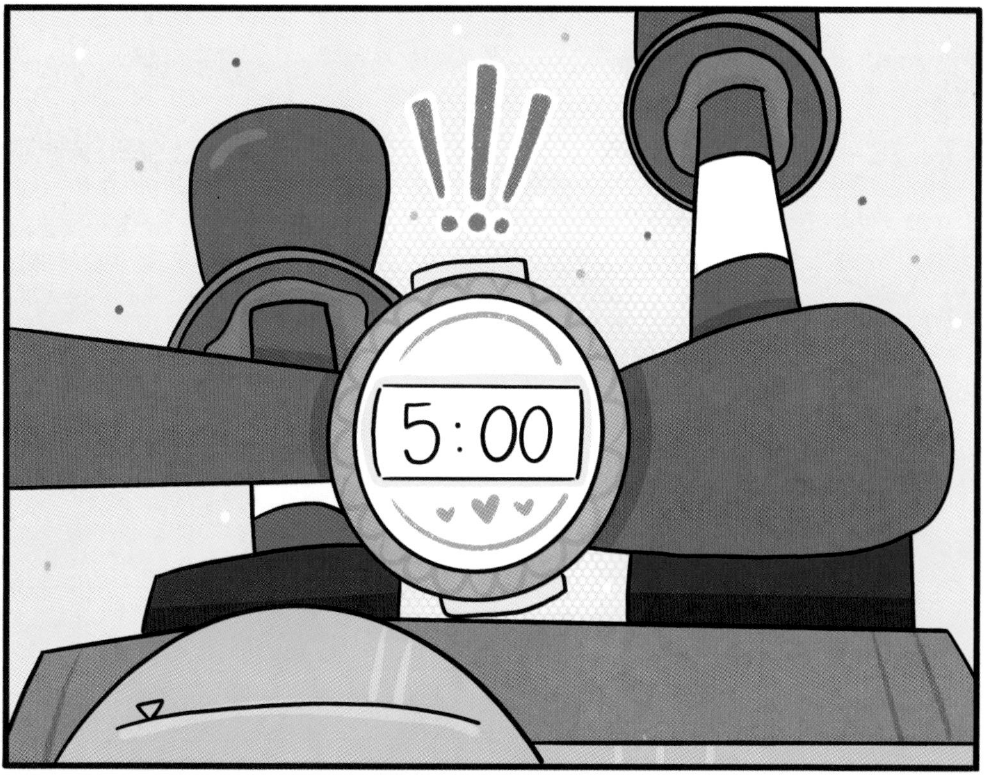
5:00

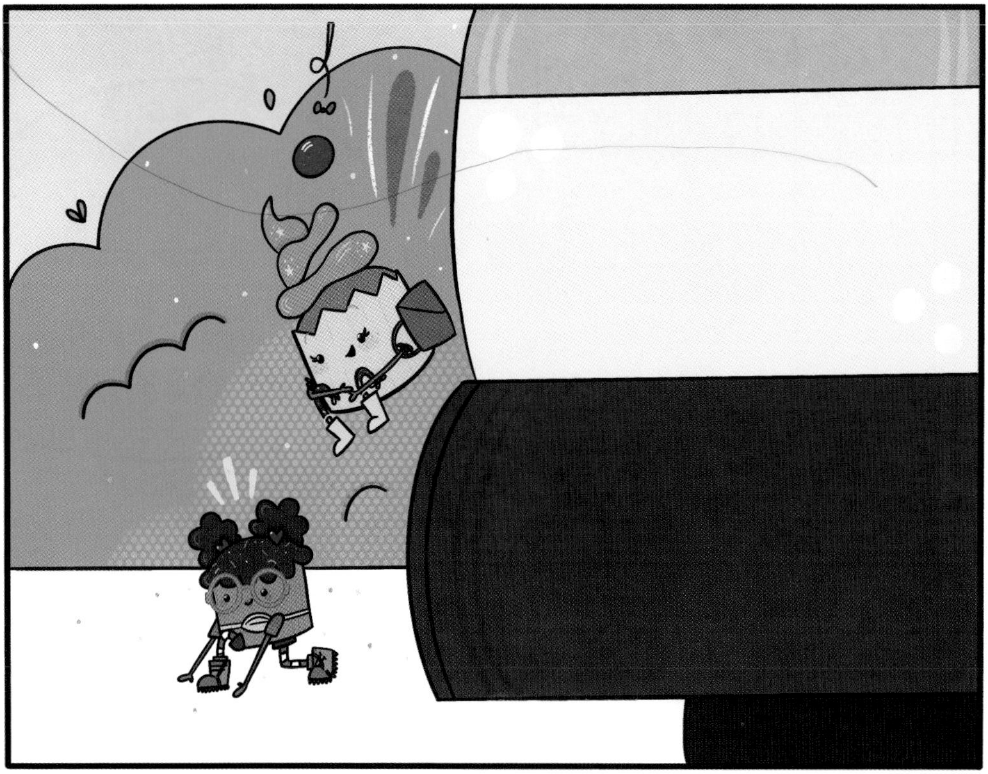

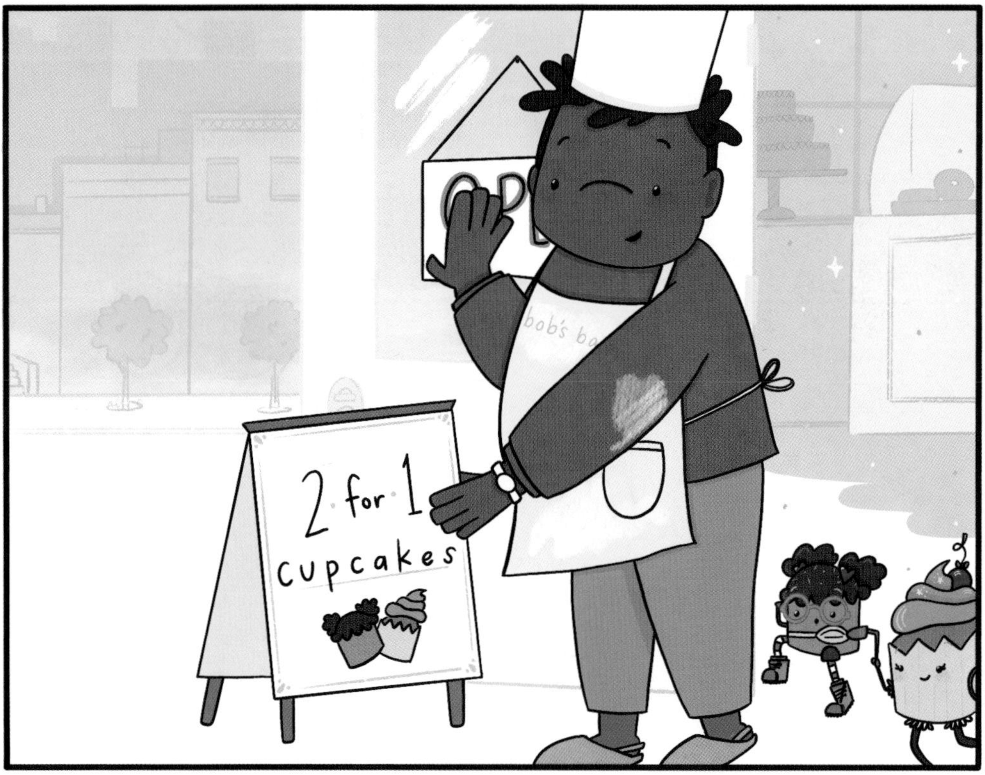
2 for 1
cupcakes

Oh, I know where we can go next!